BLOOD MOUNTAIN

BLOOD MOUNTAIN

JAMES PRELLER

FEIWEL AND FRIENDS
NEW YORK

A Feiwel and Friends Book
An imprint of Macmillan Publishing Group, LLC
120 Broadway, New York, NY 10271

Our books may be purchased in bulk for promotional, educational, or business use. Please
contact your local bookseller or the Macmillan Corporate and Premium Sales Department
at (800) 221-7945 ext. 5442 or by email at MacmillanSpecialMarkets@macmillan.com.

Library of Congress Cataloging-in-Publication Data.

Names: Preller, James, author.
Title: Blood Mountain / James Preller.
Description: First edition. | New York : Feiwel and Friends, 2019. | Summary: Thirteen-
    year-old Grace and her eleven-year-old brother Carter are watched by a mountain
    man when they get lost during a strenuous hike on Blood Mountain.
Identifiers: LCCN 2019001970 | ISBN 9781250174857 (hardcover) |
    ISBN 9781250174840 (ebook)
Subjects: | CYAC: Lost children—Fiction. | Hiking—Fiction. | Brothers and sisters—
    Fiction. | Survival—Fiction. | Hermits—Fiction.
Classification: LCC PZ7.P915 Blo 2019 | DDC [Fic]—dc23
LC record available at https://lccn.loc.gov/2019001970

Book design by Katie Klimowicz

Feiwel and Friends logo designed by Filomena Tuosto

First edition, 2019

1 3 5 7 9 10 8 6 4 2

mackids.com

This book is dedicated to my daughter, Maggie—
because when I needed inspiration
for a girl character who was fierce,
determined, sensitive, and kind,
I only thought of you.

In memory of our family dog, Daisy,
and the real Sitka of my youth.

Not till we have lost the world,
do we begin to find ourselves.

—*Henry David Thoreau*

DAY ONE

[DAY TRIP]

Blood Mountain, huh? Nice name. Very reassuring. Why do you think they call it that?" Grace asks. "Was Hell Hole already taken?"

Grace's father—a big bear of man, six two, 240 pounds with a rapidly expanding stomach, thick chest, and heavy legs—forages in the trunk of the car, hauling out hiking boots, battered backpacks, water bottles, packages of energy bars, beef jerky, trail mix, Twizzlers. He ignores his daughter or simply doesn't hear. For Grace, the distinction is meaningless. Same thing either way. He's a quiet man. Not a lot bounces back.

Perfectly balanced on the balls of her feet, Grace bends her right leg and grabs her toes, stretching one quad, then switching to the other. She ducks her head to peer into the back seat, where her younger brother, Carter, sits slumped against the far door, face pressed against the window, openmouthed. A line of drool unspools down the pane.

She whispers, "Cart, yoo-hoo, wake up, we're here, and there's blood everywhere. All over the mountain. Kind of gross if you ask me."

For an instant in his dream Carter believes his sister, imagines blood everywhere. Dark ooze—red thick rivers of sludge—every horror movie he's ever seen—

And then he awakens, brand-new, his consciousness rising up to the surface from its dark dream place like a swimmer gasping for air. Up into the light, and rise and shine, sleepyhead. He leaves behind those bloody images, doesn't even recall them now that he's awake. Carter arches his back and stretches, elbows to the car roof, fists behind his ears. He yawns, looks toward his sister with a dazed expression. Blinking, he asks, "What?"

Grace watches him, amused.

The trunk slams shut.

Carter twists around blearily, sees his father through the back window. He offers a sleepy, two-fingered wave-slash-salute.

"I see you've returned to the living," his father comments.

Carter blinks, still not fully awake. He yawns. "What time is it?"

To be exact, it is 7:23 A.M., but Grace answers only, "Time to go, bro."

Sitka, the dog, doesn't have to be told. Part shepherd, part who-knows-what, the unleashed, thick-furred, flop-eared mutt examines the edges of the forested parking area, sniffing intently, tail swishing, alert and full of energy. Here in the unpaved lot at the foot of Blood Mountain some ancient something in the dog's DNA receives signals from the wilderness, neurons firing, her inner wolf awakened. Sitka pants noisily, mouth open in what for all the world looks like a smile.

"Sitka, come," Grace commands in a voice that scarcely rises above a whisper. Instantly, the dog obeys. Sitka runs over, noses Grace's leg as if to say, "I'm here," looks up, receives a scratch on the top of the head, and circles back to check out the doings behind the open trunk of the car. The mishmash of old, new, and borrowed gear is strewn on the ground.

Mr. Taylor sits, his butt half in the trunk. His lips move as

4

he runs a finger along the free map they picked up at the motel the previous night. He's considering the trail, the distance and elevation. Vaguely remembers having hiked it years ago, but all trails blend together in the haze of memory. It won't be a walk in the park, that's for sure, but it's not rocket science, either. Just a long, hard hike. He's already insisted: "No phones. This is an internet-free day!" First they'll travel into the forest on generally level terrain, then up—not super steep, he hopes, mistakenly—and down a different trail to stop at a glacier-carved lake, then loop back to the car. Put one foot in front of the other and follow the markers. He presses against his chest with the side of his fist. Acid reflux, probably. A little indigestion. He tastes a bitter aftertaste in the back of his throat.

Mr. Taylor questions if maybe his plan is too ambitious for a day hike. They've gotten a late start. He wonders if he's physically up for it. If this is, in other words, another of life's bad ideas. They tend to pile up. But he does not wonder long. He's upstate with his two kids, a rare getaway, together in the great outdoors. Today they are going to burnish a memory. Just the three of them. A time they will always remember. His wife, their mother, wheelchair-bound and back at home, cheering on their adventure. So the father expertly folds the map accordion-style, an ancient skill, halves it lengthwise, and sets the map down on the bumper. It falls to the ground. He stoops to pick it up, shoves the map into his back pocket.

Sitka feels sure it's going to be a great day.

But what do dogs know, anyway?

[CARTER]

Carter tries, he really tries, but his father walks so painfully slow. Every fiber in Carter's eleven-year old, skinny, sinuous being shouts out, *Let's go, let's go*. He groans inwardly. They'll never get anywhere at this pace.

"Wait up," he hears Grace call. Carter turns and is discouraged to see his sister and father lagging far behind. He can tell from the look on Grace's face that she feels stuck, trapped in the role of devoted daughter, trailing behind with Dad. *Tough to be you, sister*, Carter thinks, and keeps moving.

Carter can't help himself. It's like he has rockets in his hiking boots; Carter wants to zoom along the shady trail, a dirt-and-pine-needled track with tall trees crowding in from each side. Sitka feels the same way. The dog is in thrall with animal joy, always glad to be off-leash. Sniffing under rocks, ranging wide into the underbrush, exploring off-trail, leading the way, nose to the ground, catching scents, chasing after invisible creatures, looking back imploringly, taking off again. During this early stage, the ascent is modest, if at all. The trail begins by leading them deep into the forest before, at last, taking on elevation.

Boys tend to grow in two ways. The first group grows like stems to the sun, straight up in spurts until they are tall and thin, stretched like Play-Doh from the soles of their feet to the tops of their heads, just skin and bones swimming in shapeless T-shirts.

Only later do these boys add weight to fill out their lanky frames. Other boys grow wide first, packing on extra pounds—soft and baby-faced and overfed. Only later, after growing "out," do they begin growing "up." Carter stands as a shining example of the first group. A flagpole with big feet, an untucked shirt, and a mess of blond hair sticking out from under a Dodger-blue baseball cap.

As he hikes, his body working harder now, each step demanding attention, Carter stops and grumbles and then, bored and irritable—*Let's go let's go let's go*—he feels the onward pull, starts walking again, then forces himself to sit and wait for the dawdlers. Such misery.

Finally, Carter's father relents, his face flushed, "Go on ahead, Carter. Don't let me hold you back." There is an air of irritation in his voice. Maybe a little disappointment. Then to Grace, more cheerfully, "You, too, honey. I'm good. I prefer taking it slow and steady."

[KNIFE]

The angular man carries a squirrel by the tail and lightly tosses the corpse onto a flat stone. In his right hand he holds a slingshot with a thick yellow band. Sets it aside. The sling is store-bought and he is pleased with it. He coughs once to clear his throat but does not speak. The man has not spoken in weeks. He does not keep track of traditional calendars; time for him is day and night, eat and sleep, watch the moon slice thin and then come round again. Besides, there is no one with whom to speak, and he has not yet reached the point where he converses out loud with himself. He doesn't even murmur to the birds overhead, though surely they speak to him in birdsong. No, he prefers the stillness and solitude of the deep forest. The only voices he listens to are the ones in his head.

He inspects the squirrel with a trained eye, flips it over. Rigor mortis has already begun to set in, the body stiffening, front paws curlèd as if still clinging to an invisible branch high up in the canopy. The body is still warm. A lead ball to the back of the head has done its work; the man admires the mark, a clean kill. There's dried blood around the nose and mouth, perhaps a look of surprise in the eyes. Otherwise the animal appears unharmed, gray and white with yellow coloration around the face. Even dead, a thing of terrible beauty. Like the world itself, he supposes. Maybe even more beautiful because it is dead? He muses over this; the thought troubles him, so he pushes it away like a stray branch on the trail.

There is work to do. He removes a large knife, a Rowen SE-6, from his belt holster. A bit cumbersome for this task—a sharp paring knife would do on a small animal—but he's traveled light today, leaving most of his supplies out of sight in Zone B. He has another emergency cache buried in Zone D, in addition to the main base in Zone C. After the last scare, when his camp was almost discovered by a random bushwhacker, he erased all traces of his former presence in Zone A. Rarely steps foot there anymore. And if so, lightly, swiftly. He thinks of the knife not as a weapon but as an elegant tool, designed for specific tasks. He sets the squirrel belly-down to the stone and with his left hand flips the bushy tail back over its body, pinching it firmly at the base, and slowly slices at the spot where the tailbone ends. He doesn't sever the tail completely, instead leaves it loosely attached by the outer layer of hide. With the knife tip, he expertly flicks away random fleas, inaudibly cursing each single one as he slices between meat and skin. Satisfied, he flips the squirrel to its back, grabs its rear legs with both hands, rises to step on the tail with his heavy boot, and pulls straight up. The back hide peels off until it reaches the fore-legs. Next he crouches down again and uses his fingers to probe and push between the skin and belly, separating the fur from the body until he can poke his finger clean through. He inserts the knife, sharp side up, and slices through the skin above the stomach as if cutting through holiday wrapping paper. Swift and tidy. Now the squirrel is essentially in three sections, with the creature's raw pink torso naked on the stone, the fur pulled back over the forelegs and head, the two rear legs still covered.

He pushes the elbows of the front limbs back, peeling the skin away like pulling two limbs through the arms of a tight sweater. In similar fashion, he pulls the fur off the rear legs. The body has now been stripped bare except for the head. He removes the hands and feet at the joints, the steel of his blade effortlessly slicing through cartilage. As steel meets stone, the little hands leap off with a satisfying pop. He licks his lips, allowing himself to feel hunger for the first time in days, knowing his next fresh meal is at hand. He delicately pinches the thin membrane covering the belly and makes an incision, careful not to cut into the bile sack. It takes two fingers of his left hand to open the incision. He inserts the blade, moving slowly now, careful not to cut into the entrails. He cracks the soft breastplate, slices up to the head. Now with one masterful motion, he removes the innards from the body and tosses the guts to the side. He carves away any last pieces of digestive tract, cuts through the neck to remove the head. Almost done. He removes the small glands from the armpits because, he has learned from books, they can spoil the flavor. He cleans his knife in a handful of moss, holsters it again.

Another day as far from humanity as possible.

[GRACE]

Grace thinks as she walks, tries the words out in her head:

> *The tree's leaves whisper.*
>
> *In the breeze.*

"Geez, I've gotta sneeze."

Ha, sort of a poem. The world rhymes . . . sometimes.

Thinks:

Oh bother, my brother. He so desperately wants to beat me. I'll let him push past while I pause here—water on my hip, past my lip— glug, glug, aaaaaahh. Good stuff. Cold and refreshing.

She knows she should let him win. Her mother advises it, says ever so quietly from her chair, "He needs it more than you, Grace. Carter's younger; you're thirteen. You've been winning all your life."

Grace doesn't entirely agree. One should never, ever lose on purpose. That doesn't help anyone. Just because she is good at sports, everyone assumes she has it so easy. Even her mother, who should know better.

Multiple sclerosis, I hate you.

Grace sighs, marches on.

After a long, winding ramble, deeper into the forest, the path steepens. More roots, more rocks, more sun. Harder is better. It focuses Grace's thoughts on the physical task, the movement of muscles, her power and strength. Grace tightens the straps of the

11

pack on her back to prevent it from throwing her off balance as she scrambles on all fours, pulls herself up. She wonders about Sitka and, just like that, as if summoned by the thought, the dog appears atop the rock, checking on her girl. Sitka climbs everything at least twice, up and back and up again, toggling between Carter and Grace, who wonders: *Has anybody ever strapped a Fitbit to a dog?*

Kind of a cool idea.

Her father is far behind, left in the dust, slow and steady like an old tortoise. Plodding. What's the word? Grace heard it just the other day, wrote it in her journal to remember it. Perambulation— that was it! Or walking, in other words. A perambulation in the woods. Her father's not very good at it anymore. *Father farther below. Further? Father further? Far or fur, who knows?* Grace fills her skull in this way with senseless musings while her strong, efficient body does the work. Carter out of sight, somewhere around the bend. She considers: *I should give a whistle.* But she prefers the silence or near silence. No such thing as real silence, at least not here in the wilderness. There are always sounds, creatures scurrying, the wind telling tales. Little pairs of eyes in the forest watching.

The dog returns, touches her wet nose against Grace's leg, then hurries up to Carter. *Ah, my best good dog, sweet Sitka. Hard work keeping track of the both of us. No concern for Dad. What was the song I heard? "Da-da, da-da-dum, dee-dim. God only knows . . ." The Beach Boys. Ancient surfer dudes from the way back. Sometimes Dad insists we listen to his music. Like he owns it. So, sure, knock yourself out, ancient one. That melody does stick in the head, though.*

It's nice to be out here in the mountains, climbing up and up. The body feels good, able. Like a productive run at cross-country practice.

A turnoff at some point. Sometime soon? Hmmmm. Does Carter have the map? He must; he's out front. I'll trudge on. That's what Coach said about my running the other day, "You sure can pick 'em up and put 'em down, Grace." A funny way of looking at it. But accurate. Running is a matter of fast feet. Up and down. Simple as that. Should I wait for Dad? So boring. For how long, and for what? He'll finally reach me and want to rest. An old bus named "Dad," huffing and puffing, spewing smoke out his tailpipe. Farting as he goes. Better to rocket my way to Carter, catch him up and we can wait together. Maybe get a look at that map. Hate not knowing where we're going. A lake somewhere, eventually.

Anyway, can't let him beat me. That would never be okay, no matter what Mom says.

5

[TWIZZLERS]

The ascent grows more rugged now. It requires more concentration, focus. No more wasted words. Only rarely do they pause to admire the beauty. For a long time, there's no view anyway. Forest engulfs them. Then the path turns steeply skyward. They take a step, huff, step again, up a winding stairway of rock. Sitka all business. Where earlier the dog ranged off-trail in wide arcs, up and back, nosing under scattered deadfall and into clefts and crevices, now she stays on-trail, pants when the hikers pause, conserves energy. Eyes bright, ears sharp, and nose alert all the while.

The trees grow smaller in this section, wind-beaten into bent shapes—like old people in tattered coats who push grocery carts full of plastic bags. Twigs like bony fingers. No view for hours until the path climbs in a series of strenuous switchbacks and suddenly arrives at a lookout with a view: a soul-stirring glimpse into the vastness of parkland, late summer's green undulating void.

"Wow," Carter says.

Everything and nothing.

He realizes how big it is, how gigantic.

And measured by this scale, Carter arrives at an awareness of his own smallness and deficiency. Such a big world. He's not anything yet. There's so much he doesn't know. At eleven, as much as Carter hates to admit it, he'd still lose in a fight with his sister. She's fierce. But he's closing the gap, for sure.

Soon, he thinks.

"It goes on forever," Grace says, standing at his right shoulder. "All those trees. Not a Starbucks in sight."

Carter spots an unlikely jewel, points. "There's a lake." A smudge of gray-blue in a sea of green.

"I remember one on the map," Grace says uncertainly. "That must be it?" Her intonation rises at the end, transforming a declarative sentence into a question.

"Seems far," Carter says. "Maybe that's not the one. I thought ours would be closer." He turns in a full circle, trying to absorb the entire landscape, create a map in his mind. North, south, east, west, up, down, near, far: It's meaningless now. In this imposing wilderness, he can't tell one from the other—here from there. Carter knows his shoulders ache from the pack. His feet hurt; the boots aren't broken in. There's a blister forming on his right heel.

Carter and Grace explore along the rock outcrop, past two upright halves of a split rock that towers above them. They pass over and under rocks, ledges, fissure caves. Where the path turns sharply back into the woods, they decide to rest. Carter drains the last drop of water from his metal canteen. Unshoulders his pack, lets it drop at his feet.

"What now?" he asks.

"Wait for Dad?" Grace asks. "He's carrying the sandwiches."

In answer, Carter grabs his pack by the loop strap, carries it to a nearby rock slab, sits down. He unzips the pack and pulls out a package of red Twizzlers. He pulls off two, separates them, holds one out for Grace as he bites into the other.

"At least we came prepared," Grace jokes. She sits beside him, leans back, likes it, and decides to recline on the warm, smooth rock. The sun feels good on her face; her muscles relax. Wispy clouds in the distance remind her of mares' tails. Sitka comes by, curls down beside her, snuffling her nose into Grace's ribs.

Carter finds a basic first aid kit, unzips it, extracts a Band-Aid. He considers the whole major hassle of taking off his boot, etcetera. "Grace, will you do it for me?" he asks.

Grace opens her eyes. "Seriously?"

"Blister," Carter says, just the hint of a whine in his voice. He holds out his booted foot in her direction. "Please?"

Without complaint, Grace sits up, unlaces her brother's boot, pulls it off.

"Ow," he protests.

She peels off his sock. "You're as tough as an old banana," Grace teases. She examines his sore heel, gingerly pokes the red area where the skin has ripped off. In the kit she finds pieces of precut moleskin in the shape of a doughnut, selects one, and presses it against the boy's heel. Grace is careful that no sticky part touches the raw skin. "There," she says. "That's tons better than a regular Band-Aid."

"Thanks," he replies.

She nods and leaves him to lace up his own boot.

"There's jerky in here," Carter says, holding up the bag.

Grace shrugs. "I don't trust that stuff."

"It's fine," Carter counters. He bites off a piece. "It's just dried meat."

"I don't know, it seems so . . . fake," Grace says. "Processed-food stuff, weird preservatives."

"More for me," Carter concludes.

The dog rises, comes closer to the boy, nostrils flaring, to investigate the smell.

"Here you go, Sitka." Carter sets a piece of jerky on the rock. The dog sniffs, chews thoughtfully, swallows. Steps closer, tail wagging, mouth loosely hanging open, asking for more.

"Sorry," Carter says. "Maybe later."

Grace hands a nearly full water bottle to her brother. "Pour some into my hands," she says. "Not too much. We have to make it last. Here, Sitka. Drink."

The dog laps up the cool water, tickling Grace's fingers with her whiskers and tongue.

Finally, Carter stands, restless. "Okay. I'm bored, let's get going," he announces. He accidentally drops a piece of jerky between two rocks. It's stuck there, a waste. Left for some critter to discover.

Grace yawns, blinking in the sun. It feels as if she could relax there forever. Sitka stretches, downward dog, yoga-style, moves off the rock, sniffs the breeze with an uplift of the snout, ready to explore. The dog's attention focuses primarily on the two kids, searching for signs and signals from her human companions, anticipating their next move. Grace rises to her feet, rubs the heels of her hands against her eye sockets, reaches for the sky, tippy toes. Sets off in a hurry. She calls back teasingly, "Try to keep up, Carter, if you can."

She breaks into a run, backpack and all.

6

[TROUBLE]

This hike is kicking my butt, Mr. Taylor thinks. He pauses, his right foot up on a rock, hunched over, resting his right hand on the bent knee. He tries to catch his breath. Takes a bandanna from his back pocket, mops it across his brow, the back of his neck. He can't remember ever sweating this much. He shivers at a light breeze, feels cold and clammy.

His gaze follows the trail. There's only one direction now: up and up.

He thinks:

Grace is a good girl, always looking out for her pa. She would have stayed with me the whole way. But that's what being a parent is about, right? You push them out of the nest. I couldn't hold her back. Not with Speed Racer up there, practically running up the trail. That boy, still young, only thinks of himself. Growing up takes time.

When Mr. Taylor returns the bandanna to his back pocket, his hand brushes against the trail map. Probably not great that he's the one with the map—the caboose pulling up the rear. He hopes the kids know enough to wait where the trail splits. Damn, he should have told them. But there should be markers, cairns. They'll be fine. It's not their first time on a hike. He just needs to catch his breath. Weird how his shoulders ache. Like there's a thick rope around his body, squeezing tight. Should not have eaten those burritos last night. Ah, regrets. Refried beans will repeat on a

18

guy. His chest, right at the bottom of his rib cage, feels full, tight, pressure building.

The sacrifices a father makes.

Smart to go midweek, not another soul on the trail. Nice and peaceful, far from the madding crowd. He takes a step, and another, pauses again when he feels a momentary dizziness. He massages his jawbone with his left hand. *A cavity? Loose filling? Should make an appointment with the dentist when I get back. Add it to the list. Toothaches hurt so much because they are near the brain. Great, another bill to pay, another five hundred balloons down the drain. Probably more. Doctors, bah.*

He thinks of his children, those two up there somewhere, happy on the mountain, a beautiful day. It makes him feel good. Wish they did this more, but: life. *At least I did this*, he thinks. *Hell, I made those two.* A lot of mistakes—more than he cares to count—but at least he got them right. Those two. A troubling worry persists: sure hope they have sense enough to stop where the trail splits. A moment's worry flickers across his consciousness. He gives a soft burp—burrito gas, he guesses—and determines to pick up the pace.

Up and up.

A moment later, he's throwing up on the side of the trail. *What the hell?* he wonders.

[HOLD UP]

The day gets colder, dampness clings to the air, but Grace and Carter don't notice. Sitka, of course, does—it's as plain as the nose on her face. She has no way to communicate this knowledge. But she assumes they know it, too.

"Remember what Dad would say whenever we got bad grades or did something wrong?" Grace asks Carter.

The boy laughs. "Let's walk and talk," he says.

"Yeah," Grace laughs. "There was nothing worse than getting that text from Dad. 'We need to have a walk-and-talk.'"

Carter smiles at his sister. "And every single time, we took the exact same walk."

"Past the Harts' house, around the block, and up the driveway," Grace said.

Carter puts a hand on Grace's right shoulder. In a deep, fatherly voice he says, "'I'm glad we had this chance to talk.'"

Both of them snort out loud, their voices carrying across the humps and cols of the saddleback ridge. They come to a spot that makes Carter stop. The trail seems to be vanishing before his eyes. The trees lean in, a breeze kicks up.

"Um, hold up," he says. "Shouldn't we be, like, there by now?"

[UNWORRIED]

They aren't worried yet. Not quite to the point of worry, exactly, but getting there. Their senses strain. They think harder, look closer, run calculations in their heads, assign blame, and then, suddenly, their bodies speak: hunger, thirst, weariness, and the first hint of fear.

Fear is a chemical that rushes through the veins like a flash flood after a heavy rain. Suddenly, the dam bursts and it's on top of you. A wild, rising torrent. Fear changes everything, especially the way the brain works. The brain sends out chemical signals to various body systems. Adrenaline brings blood to the skin's surface. The body begins to sweat. The heart palpitates rapidly. Muscles tighten. Breathing picks up.

"What do you think?" Carter asks.

Grace's mouth shuts. She doesn't want to look at her brother, doesn't want him to see the expression she wears on her face. She turns, searching in all directions for something, anything, a clue.

Nothing. Not a thing.

The sameness of the forest.

They have wandered off the trail but don't realize it yet. "Keep going a little farther, I guess." Grace points. "Bushwhack to that rise? Maybe we can see something."

It looks to the untrained eye to be twenty minutes away. A little down, a little up, and you're there.

Ninety minutes later, they make it, dead tired.

And the view tells them nothing.

The sudden fog obscures the details.

[HEARTBURN]

He knows he could pee right here on the trail and no one would see. But what if? Or if Grace drops back? He sure doesn't want to be caught standing out in the open. So he picks a path into the forest. His modesty brings him farther than necessary. Well out of sight. Behind a screen of dense underbrush, he finds a fat pine to take a leak against. He relishes this feeling, like being a little boy again, taking a whiz against a tree. It's fun to be outdoors, taking aim at bugs or whatever target catches his fancy. A squirrel watches from a distance, tail curled across its back. *Hey, fella, give a guy some privacy,* Mr. Taylor thinks. Zips his fly. All done.

So tired. "My get-up-and-go has gone up and went." A line from a country song he remembers. His heart beats like a drum, a reckless conga rhythm. A shiver of pain ripples down his left arm and shockingly, amazingly, he knows. All the clues come together. The dizziness, the sweats, the shortness of breath. Not heartburn, he realizes. Not old-man syndrome. Worse than that. He triangulates the distances: the kids, the car, a possible hospital, must be at least fifty miles away. Not good. His fingers tingle, the tips of his ears; vibrations sweep through his body like an ocean tide. Fast as bad news. Another shiver of electricity zings down his left arm. His eyes close, and he thinks of his children, his wife, his life, as he drops to the ground. He sees their faces. Marissa, Grace, Carter. Tough marriage, hard times, but they made such great kids together. When his head hits the rock, he no longer thinks anything at all, sleeps the dreamless sleep.

The squirrel, startled by the thump, climbs a tree.

[LOST]

They walk and bicker and walk.

Lost.

The reality of their situation presses against them, like walls closing in. A feeling of compression, of claustrophobia. Here in the middle of nowhere, without any idea whatsoever where to turn or what to do.

Carter looks to Grace for guidance, but she avoids his gaze. She appears stressed herself. Keeps running her hands from her forehead down to the bottom of her skull, pulling tight on her long brown hair. She tries to think, tries to remember every scrap of information she's ever learned and discarded. All the survival shows she's half watched on television while doing homework or texting with friends or just blowing through Instagram, bored and scrolling.

Where's Dad?

Maybe we haven't gone far enough?

Maybe we should circle back?

And if Carter hadn't been in such a hurry . . .

"Grace?" Carter says, and her name comes with a question. A sense of urgency, bordering on panic. He wants an answer.

Minutes pass. It's hard to see past twenty yards. Grace feels unsure of anything.

They are standing in a cloud. Mist envelops them. In the gathering gray, the high timber becomes a thick, dark mesh.

"We must have missed a turnoff somewhere," Grace decides. "We'll be okay. Let's just . . . figure this out."

Carter sinks to his knees, sits back on his heels. He's fried. Needs a break. His cheeks look pale, his wet hair stuck to his face in clumps. He sneezes. Sitka comes to him, made curious by the boy's behavior. The dog smells a chemical coming off Carter's skin. Licks his face. Salt, sweat, anxiety. The boy circles his arms around the dog's neck, notices her damp fur. "I'm hungry," he complains.

Grace reaches into her backpack. Hands her brother what remains of the trail mix. A few handfuls, no more. There are five energy bars left, which strikes Grace as excessive. Some instinct tells her: *Not yet.* She scours the landscape for a familiar sign: a tree, a rock ledge, anything.

But there is nothing.

It is too gray.

The fog and rain.

It all looks the same.

Grace's brain struggles to imagine where they are in relation to the parking lot, the main trail, the lake . . .

Why didn't she study the map?

Where was their father?

She shivers. The rain no longer misting but now actual drops. She has a flannel in the backpack. Carter has an extra long-sleeve T-shirt. Both are useless in wet weather. She finds one of those silver emergency blankets still in its packaging. Grace opens it and wraps it around her brother.

"We'll be okay," she tells him.

Carter doesn't quite believe it.

Grace's hand finds a small, cylindrical object. "Hey, Carter, look." She slides a button. A thin beam of light cuts into the dusky night. She waves it around like a light saber. "We're in luck. A flashlight. At least now we can see!"

Carter isn't buying Grace's cheerful act. He sits there, glum and shivering. A flashlight. Big whoop. And though she's trying hard, Grace can't quite convince herself, either. Yet she knows, down in her bones, they can't let go of hope.

11

[SLEEP TIGHT]

We can't stay here," Grace says.

Carter doesn't move. He sits with his arms around his knees, huddled in a tight ball, baseball cap pulled low on his head. He's exhausted. Grace's little brother is shutting down.

Toughen up, kid, she thinks.

"Okay, look," Grace says. "This sucks. Believe me, I know this sucks. But"—she looks to the darkening sky, rubs her neck—"we're just going to have to, like, hang tough. You know? It's going to be okay."

Movement from Carter's head. He's nodding. He hears her. Encouraged, Grace continues: "We're going to have to find some, I don't know, *shelter*. Anywhere that's dry and safe. I'm thinking we should head down, lower." She gently kicks Carter on the side of his hiking boot. "Tomorrow morning, as soon as it's light, we'll figure it out and hike out of here. By lunchtime, we'll be laughing about this with Dad."

"How are we going to find him?" Carter asks.

Grace holds out a hand before his face. Gives a little movement with the bend of her fingers, a come-on-let's-rise gesture. He reaches up, they clasp forearms, and she pulls him to standing. Grace points the flashlight at Sitka, who is watching them from the base of a nearby tree. "Let's go," she says.

28

The dog slowly comes to them, as if disbelieving, watching their eyes for instructions.

The rain picks up. Carter sneezes again.

Together, they trudge downhill through the timber, following a narrow beam of light. What they do not say, what they fail to admit, is that neither has the slightest clue where they are headed. Nevertheless, it feels good to be moving again. No matter in which direction. They are looking for an umbrella of branches, a cave, something, anything, a place to spend the night. Grace's bare arms and muscular legs feel wet and cold. She rubs them to keep warm. *It's not too bad*, she tells herself. Grace has always been goal-oriented, determined. She makes a decision, fixes on an object, and forges ahead. It's always been her way. That's Grace. The blazing arrow after its target. Now fueled by stress and emotion, that inner urge propels her, stumbling in the dark.

Sitka walks with them, staying close by, head dropping below her shoulders, ears keen to any sound.

"Slow down," Carter finally says.

Grace stops. "What?"

Carter pauses, blinks. "Let me see that flashlight."

He sweeps the flashlight in a slow circle, like a lighthouse on a rocky shore. It settles on a massive tree trunk that lies fallen. Near the upturned root, the trunk is a foot above the ground and stretches out at least fifty feet in a clean line.

"There," Carter says.

"What do you mean?" Grace asks. She wants to keep moving.

"That's where we're going to wait this out," Carter says. "Under that log."

"Carter . . . ," Grace begins.

"You're leading us nowhere," Carter says. "I'm tired, Grace. I'm hungry. This is beyond stupid." He points to Sitka, already on the ground, her head resting on her front paws. He bends to touch the dog's head. "Even Sitka needs a break."

They walk toward the fallen tree. "Feel this," Carter says. "Still dry. And there's moss. Maybe we could—"

"Make a bed," Grace says. "There's a knife in your backpack. Check the side pockets to see if there are any matches."

"I checked already," the boy responds.

"Check again."

"No," Carter retorts, irritated. "Do you think I'm an idiot? Like I don't *want* to find matches? Like I haven't looked a dozen times already? Do you think I want to be here with you, wet and cold and . . ." He runs out of steam. He knows this isn't helping. They are both too fried to argue. So Grace cuts and gathers the boughs of a hemlock. Tries to shake the rainwater off. Carter shovels out a small depression beneath the log with his hands, tossing away loose sticks and rocks. He gathers clumps of dry moss, nature's mattress. Together, they make it as soft as they can.

They lie down, huddle close, sharing the small emergency blanket. Head to head, toe to toe. The ground is, amazingly, not terrible. Sitka moves off to a nearby spot, curls up. After a few minutes, at Grace's invitation, the tired dog presses into them for warmth.

A crack of thunder makes the earth shake. The rain comes down harder, but at least they are somewhat protected. A few giants of the woods fall in the night, great branches crashing to the ground. Grace reaches out to hold Carter's hand.

"I'm glad we have the knife," she whispers. "Try to sleep."

Carter is too exhausted to answer. He gives a soft moan. In his heart, he feels that it's going to be bad. Something awful, something terrible, is going to happen. And there's nothing he can do about it. He lies awake, staring into the darkness. He senses a twitch in Grace's leg. His sister has fallen asleep.

[STEALTH]

The angular man, all long levers and pointy elbows and bushy beard, moves in the same way that fog descends into a valley—softly, silently, gently. He leaves no trace, practiced in the art of invisibility. Here and then, a wisp of cloud, gone. A vapor, vanished. "Good walking leaves no tracks." It's a line he has starred and underlined in his favorite book, a dog-eared, ragged copy of *Tao Te Ching*, a book of philosophy attributed to the Chinese poet Lao Tzu.

To be seen is loss, is lack, is jail, is death. Thus he leaves no tracks, moves primarily at nightfall, a headlamp switched to low beam when necessary, his clothes dark, his face and hands caked with mud. A penlight hangs on a chain around his neck, tucked under his shirt, as a backup should the headlamp fail. The big knife strapped to his belt. He threads the forest with graceful precision, turns and twists his torso, swivels and seeks out rocks, avoids making footprints in mud. He fears that one random print might give him away. So he moves like a cat: doesn't break a twig, flatten a fern, or kick a mushroom.

He travels swiftly, quick but unhurried, racing the approaching light of dawn. He returns from another night raid. The burgled haul rolled snug in his heavy backpack, necessary items for his survival. In exchange, he leaves what cash he can. The monthly checks deposited directly into his account, retrieved through heart-pounding excursions to an obscure ATM, hood pulled low to hide his face from the security cameras. The raids leave him with twinges of guilt. He was tempted, once, to leave a note of apology, but not foolish enough to follow through with it. He does no harm, leaves few clues. However, he does not consider it stealing, in the strictest sense. Or, truthfully, he does not *consider it* at all. Not anymore. The man has learned not to think too much. No peace there. He's cultivated quite the opposite—the emptiness of thought, the silence of the bending willow by the water, his world stripped to essentials. Roots drink deep. The crown climbs to light. Why haunt the night with thoughts? He is as solitary as any soul in this world, a hermit in his garden, contemplating nothing. His suffering has pulled him inward, a doodlebug rolled into a protective ball.

The dividing line between forest and figure evaporates on these silent treks back to Zone C, and it is here where he loses himself completely—the witching hour when he feels, at last, and only fleetingly, unburdened. Walking in trackless stealth. By pulling inward into his suffering, he creates an orderly world of temporary calm and peace.

A clenched fist of sorrow.

There is no other way.

He simply exists in this wilderness, thinking of batteries and propane and waterproof clothes and tea bags and jelly beans and nuts and oats and the harsh winter ahead. He wishes to be deleted. Erased. To be: no one. Not death, but deathless. The deepest, safest solitude. And here, in momentary lapses, gliding through the ghostly forest, he succeeds. He is a man who can no longer remember his name. *John, is it?* He persists; he endures; he fades into the landscape and disappears. A shadow among shadows, dissolved into a northeastern forest dominated by mixtures of maple, birch, beech, spruce, hemlock, fir, and pine.

A flashlight's pale beam attracts his attention. The man who never sleeps, who stalks this land in the darkest hours, instinctively stoops to his haunches. He stares across at the distant beam of light. His pulse slows. The beam disappears through the trees and returns again, revealed in a momentary break between trees. The light's progress, he judges, is at the pace of an individual walking slowly through the woods. The light comes from the ridge across the way. The man does not move, nor does he make a sound. Something inside him activates, like a flame roaring to life. Another part of him seals off, turns black. He watches the flickering, fading light and becomes the predator.

A hiker, he surmises. *But at this hour? Over there? A strange place to camp.*

Another thought: *A possible threat?* His throat feels dry. In slow, precise movements, he unscrews the cap of his water sack, drinks enough to wet his lips and throat. *Are they after me?* he wonders. *Have I been discovered?* He moves to a better position. Climbs an easy tree with low branches. He watches until the light dies out. He marks the spot in his mind. Fixes it with his compass. Then he climbs down and sets off in the dark to gather facts. His mission: to move unseen, to scout and patrol the sector, to assess the tactical situation, and respond accordingly. The basics of observation, drilled into him from another world, a lifetime ago. The time he's tried to forget. The memories carved into his bones. He instinctively reaches for his right hip, feels the knife in its holster, heads out.

13

[MAKAYLA]

Makayla Devaroix awakens in the dark of her modest cabin to the sound of the alarm. Rise and blur. But first, coffee. A strong pot. Her mind is cobwebs. Even the sun doesn't want to get up. Makayla is twenty-seven years old, with smooth brown skin and wavy black hair. Her brows are thick and striking above gray eyes. Fit and strong, she moves with an athlete's economy and grace. She cleans the filter, pours the water, spoons the coffee grounds without thought; she could do this in her sleep and practically does. She sits on a low stool by the coffee machine, watching as it fills. She lives alone, does not own a television. The laptop is enough for podcasts, Spotify, and the occasional romantic comedy.

Yesterday had been a long, hard day, and today looked like it would be worse. She had gotten the call sometime around 2:00 A.M. from dispatch: A kayaker had gone missing out by a string of ponds off Paradise Lake. Makayla double-checked the map. It would take an hour in her patrol vehicle just to get close. She'd meet up with another ranger at the pull-off. They'd split up and begin a basic type 1 search. There were tributaries to cover, plus the kayaker might have carried his boat, or portaged, a short distance between navigable waters. The kayaker had been alone, an experienced backpacker, but had failed to return home as expected.

Probably it was nothing. Or maybe he ran into real trouble out there. No matter what, it could take a full day to find the answer.

If the body is discovered at the bottom of the lake, which is a thing that sometimes happens to bodies out here in parkland, it would require state police scuba divers and more gear and a whole lot more coffee to close this sad chapter. Makayla never got used to the sight of hauling a body out of the water, the skin gone gray, the eyes and lips eaten away by fish. With staff cuts and slashed budgets, Makayla spends most of her week chasing emergencies: lost hikers, injured adventurers, drowned teenagers, and wildfires. It's simple math. The park is getting more crowded than ever before, particularly in the popular parts, with fewer rangers to cover the more remote territory. More and more people come in, knowing less and less. Impossible to do the job right. She'd seen flip-flops on mountaintops, hikers shivering from frostbite wearing only shorts and a T-shirt, clueless as to how to read a simple compass. Dumb as a box of nails. Most egregious to Makayla, they failed to respect the mountains. She finished her cup with a long gulp, poured the remainder of the pot into a travel mug, laced up her boots, and headed out.

This was her dream job. The city girl who majors in environmental science and forestry in college—discovers she loves it, *needs it*—and decides to become a ranger. Still true, though harder, and lonelier, than she ever imagined.

[RISE, SHINE]

Carter sits on a rock, pulls on his boots, grimaces uncomfortably as he tightens the laces. His neck, back, shoulders, hips all ache from a long, damp night on the unforgiving earth. If he slept, he doesn't remember it. Spider bites cause small, red welts on his torso—his body injected with microdoses of poison. Enough to kill a fly. The itching drives him crazy.

He decides to let Grace sleep. She surely didn't get much during the night. On the stupid ground. Under a crummy log. Whose idea was that? *Oh, his.*

Misery.

The hollowness in his gut gives him a carved-out sensation. He can't remember being this hungry before. Carter thinks of all the times he sat down to dinner, announcing, "I'm starving!" Now he realizes it was a dumb thing to say. Starving in a house full of food. He imagines a stack of pancakes, butter, maple syrup, bacon. Maybe, if things go right, he'll order some in a roadside diner later today.

He remembers the Twizzlers in the pack and eats the last two. Carter knows he should have saved one for Grace, and intended to, but it tasted so good. Before he realized it, the second one was in his mouth. Oh well! The morning is overcast, but the fog has retreated and it's stopped raining. He switches out his damp Nike shirt for the dry, long-sleeved one. He's not cold anymore, but he's not warm, either. Looks up to find the sun. It's shrouded by clouds. Somewhere up there, he surmises, where the gray seems lighter. He remembers: the sun rises in the east and sets in the west. Good to know, though he's not exactly sure in what way that might be useful information. He suppresses the feeling that he is nowhere. That somehow they've wandered into a void, never to be seen again.

Sitka noses around in the bush, claws at the dirt, intent on something. The dog seems happy enough. Maybe a little wilder in some ways, transformed here in the great outdoors. Hopefully she can scavenge something. Carter understands that they'll need water. And soon. He believes Grace still has some in her pack. It's by her feet. He decides to wait. He notices that the trees have come alive with the morning light. Birds sing, chirp, tweet, cheep— flitter from branch to branch. A chipmunk appears, turns left, right, pauses, scurries away. Carter wonders how it would taste. Pretty gross, he guesses. He isn't *that* hungry.

Grace groans, sits up dazedly. She rubs her eyes, yawns. Her hair a comical tangle of knots. Sitka comes over, sniffs Grace's hands, face. As if to say: *Just checking*.

"Morning," Carter says.

Grace's head swivels. Her eyes widen to focus. She blinks, half smiles. "You're up."

Carter doesn't answer.

"How'd you sleep?" Grace asks.

Carter's lips tighten. He shakes his head.

Grace stands up and stretches. Arms wide, arms to the sky, back arched. Hands to hips, she twists, spreads her feet wide, touches the ground with her palms, finishes it off with a few standing jumps. Trying to wake her body up, get the blood flowing. She reaches for the bottle of water, gives it a shake, not much in there. She takes a small swig. Offers the bottle to her brother. "Want some?"

He opens his hands like a wide receiver, and she tosses the bottle underhand. He catches it and drinks. Then asks, "Can I finish it?"

Grace nods.

Bottoms up.

"So," Carter says. "We survived."

Grace smiles. "We did, didn't we?"

"What's the plan?" he asks.

Grace yawns, loudly and deeply. "I've been thinking about that all night. We should, I guess . . ." Grace turns, head still foggy, seeking a familiar sight, anything to get her bearings. It all looks so dense and green, cleansed and fresh, different from the previous night. A tide of unease washes over her, as Grace realizes she doesn't actually know which way to go. In the dark, thinking it over, it seemed clear. They'd wake, start walking, find a trail . . .

"Which way, you think?" she asks.

"I was following you," Carter points out, accusation in his voice.

Grace doesn't like it. "You were checked out last night, sitting in the rain. We needed to get dry."

"Okay, so . . ." Carter stands, almost randomly points. "What about that way?"

"We need water," Grace says.

"Yes," Carter replies.

He waits for their next move.

"I guess if we keep heading down," Grace says, gesturing. "We'll eventually come across a brook or stream."

Carter stands, arms crossed. He's already toast, and the day has barely begun. "Makes sense, I guess."

"What do *you* think, Sitka?" Grace asks.

The dog comes over, prancing a little, head tilted, flop ears lifted, considering the question. They lock eyes, the girl and her dog. Grace bends and scratches the animal all over her head, neck, and lower back. The dog doesn't quite surrender to this affection as she would on a winter evening on a rug by the fire. Sitka is somehow—in a manner Grace can't quite pinpoint—slightly less domesticated than she was two days ago. Less pet, more dog. "Maybe *you* can find water for us, huh?" Grace asks, voice rising in a singsong manner. Sitka's chest thrusts forward, the two front paws lift off the ground, come to rest on Grace's bent knee, yaps once, pants warm breath into her face.

"Let's do this," Grace says.

They set off. Stiff-bodied, putting one foot in front of the other. They move farther from where they started. Deeper into the sprawling parkland. Hurrying off, slipping on damp roots and wet leaves, determinedly going in the wrong direction.

[DOWNHILL]

The process of getting lost—truly, bewilderingly lost—is a curious endeavor. But first, consider the word *bewildered*. Confused, disoriented. Tangled, clouded, dazed, befuddled. To be made *wild*, untamed, *wildered*. To become, yourself, wilderness. And thus: *bewildered*. It's not instantaneous. There's nothing "suddenly" about it. You have to venture off the beaten path. The hikers don't realize it at first. Not fully. Sure, they may suspect. Disquieting thoughts might worm into their minds, but those thoughts are pushed aside. A day ago they were sitting in a dandelion-colored Volvo. How lost could they be?

That's step one. Denial.

And so for the next few hours Grace and Carter cling to the idea they are not *really* lost, not *really* in a world (a turned-around, upside-down whirled!) of trouble. *The solution is just up ahead, around the next bend.* They quicken their pace, push harder to get there, eager to arrive somewhere, anywhere, that's not this bewildering wilderness of lostness.

And yet, and yet.

There comes a moment of recognition. Carter already knows on a gut-deep level. They are hopelessly, deliriously lost. He's known since the crack of dawn, though he wished he were wrong. Put his faith in his sister. Grace has always been really smart. A top athlete; a track star. Not easily defeated. There's no "give up" in Grace Taylor.

They spend a grueling day trekking downhill. Slipping, steadying. There are moments of optimism. They find a narrow drainage stream, high-five, and fill their water bottles. Sitka stands in cool water and laps noisily. Rejuvenated, they decide to follow it down because, they hope, it should lead somewhere. A road or lean-to or something. Instead, they pull wearily up to a grim, gray bog with dead, leafless trees. Something stronger than worry tugs at Grace. She wonders for the first time about their survival. She had accepted "lost," but with it had always assumed "found" would be the only possible conclusion. But now a new thought crosses her mind: *Will they get out of this alive?*

Grace doesn't know the answer.

Carter slaps at a mosquito on his neck. Then at his legs and arms. He furiously claws his knees.

"Carter, stop," Grace says. "You're making yourself bleed."

He stares at her, seething, then viciously slaps the back of his neck. "Where are we?" he says, tossing each word as if it were a live grenade. There's no view at all, just a tangle of trees, swamp, and low brush. They have succeeded only in getting themselves deeper into the lowlands of the unwelcoming forest.

Grace sees that Carter's tottering on the edge. He's tired and frustrated and frightened. It's as if the dank bog itself has reached up and stolen away his spirit. Grace steps toward her younger brother. "Hey, I know. It's this muddy, gross swamp. Flies and mosquitoes everywhere." Grace shrugs off her backpack, pulls out the first aid kit. "Let's move away from here—back that way, where the bugs aren't so bad—I think there's some aloe in here. It will help with the itching."

"Is there any bug spray?" he asks.

Grace doesn't reply—and Carter takes that as her answer. He reaches into the bog and pulls out a handful of black muck. He rubs it on his legs. He takes two handfuls and covers his arms and neck.

"Smart," Grace says. "Animals do this, right? Like, hippos and stuff? Pigs and elephants?" She begins slopping mud all over her skin, including her face. It feels like a small victory.

"Beats getting eaten alive," Carter says.

"Yeah, good thinking," Grace says.

They walk back in the direction from where they came. At fifty yards distance, they stop.

"You okay?" she asks.

"Yeah." He nods. Looks at her. There's new resolve in his eyes. "It's just . . ." He doesn't finish his sentence. There's no need.

"This was a mistake," Grace admits. "It's like we came down the wrong side or something."

Carter looks up at the steep incline ahead of them. Back the way they came.

"It sucks, but I think we have to—"

"Go back up," Carter agrees.

"I just think if we can, like, get to a summit where we can see," Grace says. "Then maybe."

Carter's face is covered with muddy streaks, pale semicircles under his eyes. He looks thin, undernourished. Even the dog, Sitka, seems spent. Grace considers the five energy bars she has tucked away in her pack. *Not yet*, she decides. Maybe later she can "find" one without revealing the entire stash. Instead, they drink water. "We have no choice," Grace states. "You going to be okay?"

"Like you said, there's no choice," Carter retorts. He turns and takes the lead, bushwhacking back up the hill, following the drainage rock bed, hoisting themselves up by using branches and slender, young trees.

"Hey, look," Grace says. "A frog."

They pause to look at it. The small frog jumps once, twice. Sitka lunges for it, bites and chomps three times, swallows.

"Oh, that's so gross, Sitka!" Grace yelps.

Carter pats the dog's hips admiringly. "Good job, Sitka," he says. "Now find me a hamburger."

"With cheese," Grace adds.

"And bacon!" Carter snorts.

They continue their arduous trek, heads pitched forward, eyes focused on the ground. Grace allows Carter to set the pace, content to follow. She internally recites a little four-line poem in rhythm to their steps.

No food, no place, no here, nowhere.

She says it over and over again.

Step by step.

No food.

No place.

No here.

Nowhere.

No food no place no . . .

And then through a break in the canopy, a shaft of sunlight slices to the earth like a silver sword. Grace looks up: a patch of blue sky. Bluer than she's ever seen before. And beyond that, the jagged outline of a ridge.

"See that?" she squeals. "That's what I'm talking about, Carter! We're almost there! You're awesome—you know that? You are freaking awesome!"

An unexpected surge of adrenaline comes over her. Grace starts bouncing like a rabbit, bounding from rock to rock, joyous and giddy, slipping and falling and laughing. Sitka joins in for the first time all day, mouth open, bounding excitedly, too. She barks, a couple of short, sharp, playful yaps. Pounds the ground with two front forelimbs, butt high, tail wagging.

[RECONNAISSANCE]

The hikers don't seem to know where they are going, which makes them challenging to follow. Hard to predict in their obliviousness. Hiking through the bush, deeper into the wilderness, farther from roads or the lake or the main trails. Makes no sense.

On the other hand, they are clumsy and loud, breaking sticks and crashing through branches, talking, sneezing, complaining.

They are, he realizes, two lost kids.

And a dog.

The dog presents a difficulty. An obstacle to overcome.

He knows they could surely die. People make mistakes out here, and nature does not forgive. Not his problem. But they may bring searchers, dogs, helicopters. The chopping sound he still hears in his dreams, the bird's blades churning the air. The more pressing issue is they appear to be wandering into Zone D, not far from a buried cache of supplies. He does not want the attention.

He pulls on his beard abstractedly, deep in rumination. He's like a cow masticating on the side of the road, pondering life's infinite possibilities. The boy reminds him of someone. A broken body from a faraway land. The man pictures a boy kicking a ball in the dusty streets. Laughing, smiling.

He shakes those sun-hazed memories from his mind, grazes on a pocket of dried fruit and almonds. How long can these kids keep up their energy? Can't have much food. Fear and panic will carry you only so far. Mistake upon mistake upon mistake.

He wonders, *What to do, what to do?*

He decides on nothing.

Nothing is often best.

Trust nature. Let it take its course. It could be they'll remain forever lost. They've already strayed far off any maintained trails. Mistakenly followed a deer track for too long, lost their way and kept going.

Lost.

The word sings to him: *lost, lost!*

Lost is a state of being.

Lost is a place in his dream.

The last, lost world.

Escape from everything.

Until the self evaporates.

He loses his name, his attachments, his burdens.

He lives no place and every place.

Finally free.

He munches on a dried apricot. The park is so big, a million places to hide. Maybe the searchers won't ever find them, not a trace, not even their sun-bleached, scattered bones.

He pops an almond into his mouth. He decides to head back to his main camp, catch up with these two tomorrow. The way they walk, at this meandering pace, it won't be hard to pick up their trail.

Sleep tight, he wishes to the wandering, mud-streaked urchins. *Don't let the bedbugs bite.*

[FALL]

Fueled by wild hope and a weird kind of ecstasy, Grace and Carter attack the slope and climb, climb, climb. It is wearying and difficult, yet somehow the vision of that uppermost ridge, backed by blue sky, has revitalized them. Nearing the top, just twenty more yards to go, Grace accelerates.

And she's off, scrambling recklessly on hands and feet, creating her own pathway over loose stones, rock slabs, and dirt. She arrives first. Sitka at her feet. Carter instantly sees it in her face. Bewilderment, disappointment. They have reached a false summit. There is no magical view, no golden road to lead them back home. Grace looks like a kid who didn't receive a promised gift for her birthday. No shiny new bicycle after all.

Carter slips on a slick rock, bangs his knee. He looks up, and she is waving to him. No, her arm is rising, reaching. Grace is tilting, leaning away from him. The expression on her face is one of surprise at the moment it disappears from view.

"Grace!" he cries.

Carter reaches the top in seconds, propelled by sheer panic. He sees Grace tumbling down a scree of loose rocks. Her weight carries her backward. Thirty feet down the steep slope, Grace blasts through a tangle of plants and scrawny bushes. Sitka bounds after her, as if it's a game. Grace crashes into and off a large boulder. There is a muffled cry and the meaty sound of flesh meeting rock, followed by the crack of bone on stone. Grace's arms desperately reach for air, thrashing like a drowning swimmer, her hand reaches for the trunk of a tree, fails to hold its grip. She rolls in somersaults, trying to find some purchase, anything to slow her downward trajectory. Her heels kick in the air, her foot gets snared in the cleft between two rocks, her head bounces, her eyes roll back into her skull and ligaments shred; she keeps hurtling hopelessly downward. Sitka follows, barking. Carter sees there's a ledge below, the edge of a parched waterfall, and Grace is a river that spills helplessly to the edge . . . and Grace screams . . . and she's gone.

18

[GRACE]

Carter hears the muffled, meaty thud a moment later.

"Grace!" he cries.

A silence that lasts a lifetime. In reality, just a second or two. And then she calls back to him—not words, not instructions. The sound of a wounded animal, piercing the air.

Sitka scrambles to the edge, looks down, prepares to leap.

"Sitka, no!" Carter commands. He follows behind, crabwalking feetfirst, careful not to lose his traction. "I'm coming!" he calls to Grace.

The dog bolts to the right, circling down and around. Near the edge, Carter glances down. Grace is sprawled on the ground below, a distance of less than fifteen feet, but a long way to fall. There's blood on the rock near her head, which is turned to the side. Grace's right foot seems turned in an unnatural way. She doesn't move. Carter follows Sitka's path.

Sitka arrives, nosing her, licking Grace's face, pacing anxiously, whining.

Carter finds a way down, leaps the final five feet, rolls to the ground. He stands paralyzed for a few seconds, staring at her. "Grace?" he says.

He doesn't know what to do.

Her eyes open; she nods her head. "I'm okay," she says. "Just a little . . ." Her eyes close. Her face contorts in pain.

Carter kneels at her side, takes her head in his hands, pushes loose strands of hair from her face. He scans her body. Her ankle looks bad. Her arms and legs are scratched and bloodied. There's a deep gash on the meaty part of her right calf, a chunk of loose flesh hanging off. He touches it, pushes the skin more or less back in place. A large bruise is already forming on the side of her face. He gently probes it with the tips of his fingers, wondering if her cheekbones might have been shattered. Grace's bottom lip is cut, already swollen. She wheezes, coughs, reaches across her stomach. "My ribs," she says. She coughs again, turns her head, spits blood.

"You're alive," he says.

Grace gives the softest of snorts. Her eyes close and open. She nods. "So far," she says. She spits again. A small blob of blood. There's a taste on her tongue she can't place. *What is it?* Grace wonders. Not saliva, not blood. Something else, something bitter, the aftertaste of panic.

Carter repeatedly strokes her hair, nervous and afraid. His fingertips lightly touch her nose, her eyelashes, her face. "I saw you go over . . . ," he says, shaking his head. A shiver causes his body to tremble. "Oh, Grace."

"I'm okay," she says in a fragile, timorous voice. She laughs, moans, and spits again. "Just, you know, maybe you can get the first aid kit. Start patching me back together again."

[ESCAPE]

Wi-Fi is spotty at best in parkland, and nonexistent in remote sections, so rangers commonly communicate via portable radios. Before climbing back into her patrol vehicle, a massive Ford Super Duty F-250 truck, Makayla reports to her immediate supervisor, Lieutenant Frank Watkins. Frank is a good guy with a big job. Like the conductor of a sprawling orchestra, Frank stays abreast of all ranger activities over a vast, five-million-acre park.

"So how you doing this afternoon?" Frank asks in his cheerful, grandfatherly manner. "That was good work you did today."

Makayla smiles. "Yes, a good outcome."

Frank says, "You must be beat. When's the last time you took a day off?"

"Don't start," Makayla warns. "I don't want to think about it."

"Okay, Brooklyn. So what's next on your agenda?" Makayla grins to herself. Frank always called her Brooklyn, ever since he got wind of her city roots. A world away. Fire hydrants and apartment complexes. Concrete and people everywhere. "Depends if you've got anything for me, Frank. We're done here, safe and accounted for. I thought I'd check in on a few campsites on my way back. Call it a day." She adds, "There's been reports of bear activity. And campers get sloppy."

"Some do," Frank replies. "Look, we're all overworked and

understaffed. But you are trying to do the work of three rangers. Just do what you can, Brooklyn—I can't ask for more than that. Hey, none of that's why I called. Did you happen to hear about the trouble down in the valley? It was on TV today."

"I don't watch much television," Makayla reminds her supervising ranger.

"Well, shoot, I'd be lost without my baking shows," Frank says. He is deadly serious about his apple cobbler.

In the driver's seat, Makayla checks the rearview mirror. She flips a switch, puts the radio on speaker, shifts into reverse, executes a three-point turn out of there. "Do I have to beg, Frank? Or are you going to tell me what was on TV?"

"You sitting down for this?"

"I'm in the truck, Frank. I always sit down when I drive," Makayla jokes.

"So there's this fellow named Ernest Billingsworth. One of those well-heeled gentleman farmers. You know what I'm saying? Wall Street type, made a killing managing hedge funds, retired young. He bought a nice chunk of land up here. Turns out, Mr. Ernest Billingsworth has a thing for exotic animals."

Makayla shakes her head. "Oh no, I can see where this is going."

"I bet you can't," Frank replies. "Because our friend Ernest especially likes big cats. Cheetahs, panthers, mountain lions. He has his own private zoo in a barn behind the main house."

"Did something happen to those animals?" Makayla asks.

"You sound more worried about the animals than poor Mr. Billingsworth," Frank says.

Makayla doesn't deny it.

"It appears one of his mountain lions got loose," Frank says.

"Get out!" Makayla exclaims.

"Yep. The cat's flown the coop."

"How'd that happen?" Makayla wonders.

She could almost hear Frank shrug through the airwaves. "I'd ask Mr. Billingsworth personally, but he got his skull crushed. That's how they kill, you know. A mountain lion bites its prey at the base of the skull. They have very powerful jaws. It's impressive. Can crush bones the way I'd crumple a red velvet cupcake."

"Where's the lion now?" Makayla asks.

"That's the main thing," Frank replies. "Nobody knows. It's out, footloose and fancy-free. The cage door was open when the police got there."

Makayla drives the narrow dirt road, jostled by ruts and bumps, thinking it over. "So you're saying there's a mountain lion somewhere around here—could be near town, could be up in the mountains—and it's already killed a man?"

"That's the size of it," Frank answers. "The story gets worse."

"Worse?"

"That lion breakfasted on a fair-size chunk of Mr. Billingsworth's intestines and inner right thigh. Must've been hungry. Or maybe that wild cat just didn't like being owned. So, yeah, it has tasted human flesh."

Makayla was familiar with stories of illegal pet owners. They were sprinkled all over the country. Strange types who often didn't know what they were getting into, didn't have the resources or temperament to properly care for the animals. Amateur zoo-keepers. Idiots, every one. She didn't feel too badly about the fate of Ernest Billingsworth. "Any signs of cruelty?"

"Well, I suspect so. Undernourished, abused. We got a Humane Society rep over at the place now, taking inventory. She's got to organize transfers to authorized zoos and whatnot. We've put all the available hounds on the cat, a crew of our best volunteers, even aviation assistance, but I'm not optimistic. The first priority has to be with the security of the local community. People are mainly worried about livestock and pets and small children on backyard swing sets. The mayor is screaming. I suspect that cat will head for the hills. They don't call 'em mountain lions for nothing."

Makayla sighs. "You need anything from me?"

"No, we got this covered," Frank says. "So, Brooklyn, you've got your gun, of course?"

Makayla's eyes reflexively go to her hip holster. "You bet."

Frank says, "Be extra careful out there if you're running trails. We've put out a general alert, but it's an enormous park. These cats don't generally attack people . . ."

"But you never know," Makayla replies.

"Nope, you don't," Frank agrees. "A woman got killed by a cougar in Oregon not long ago. It happens. There's no knowing what this mountain lion will do out in the wild." His tone changes, becomes more urgent. "You come across it, Brooklyn, don't hesitate. Take it down. A mountain lion's not going to wait around for you to make up your mind."

"I won't think twice," Makayla says, nodding to herself as she drives. "Keep me posted, Frank."

"Sure thing," Frank said.

"Thanks, old man," Makayla replied. "Don't get too fat sitting behind that desk all day."

"I walk to the coffeepot six times daily for exercise," Frank says, rubbing his belly.

"And no doughnuts," Makayla orders.

"Too late!" Frank chortles.

"Okay, catch you later."

"Over and out," he answers, and clicks off.

That's what Makayla loved about her impossible job. There was always something new.

Where in the world could that big cat be now?

A mountain lion wandering free in the wilderness, likely for the first time in its life. Just a matter of time before it kills again. They are intensely private animals, rarely spotted in the wild. Makayla had read about isolated attacks on humans in the past, but few and far between. The attacks were most often on children. The experts figured that the mountain lions mistook the children for small prey.

But this one here? It had already killed a man. If it has been mistreated, Makayla theorizes, this mountain lion might not like humans very much. She takes a deep breath. It might go after a camper or hiker.

She remembers a story out of Zanesville, Ohio. Maybe ten years back. The owner of an exotic-animal park had killed himself, but not before releasing almost sixty animals, including a grizzly bear, a baboon, a bunch of monkeys, more than ten lions, and eighteen rare Bengal tigers. Beautiful animals. A crew of sheriff's deputies with high-powered rifles spent the night gunning them down. A slaughter. Had to be done, but the thought of it gave Makayla a sick feeling in her stomach. *Some people are the absolute worst*, she thinks.

[FIRST AID]

Carter pulls out the first aid kit. He makes a rapid study of its contents: sterile wipes, Advil, Band-Aids, moleskin, tweezers, a pair of small scissors, a whistle, aloe vera, butter-fly bandages, hydrogen peroxide, ChapStick, Q-tips, square gauze pads, and a roll of gauze wrap. Also: superglue and duct tape.

Not bad. He silently thanks his father for preparing the kit.

He gives Grace the water bottle, props up her head with one hand as she sips. "I have Advil," he offers.

Grace rubs a hand across her forehead. "I think," she begins, falters, tries again. "Doesn't that thin the blood? I remember some-thing like that from track. Or maybe that's aspirin?"

"So?" he says.

"It's just, if there's internal bleeding," Grace says. "I don't think you're supposed to—"

"Oh." Carter sits there, feels dumb, useless. "I've got these wipes," he says. "I should clean you up. Right? I mean, that's what Mom always did when we scraped a knee." And so he bends over his sister, dabs gently, wipes away the blood. He inspects the cut on the back of her head. A bump, the size of a robin's egg, has already formed. "The cut isn't bad. Weird there's so much blood." He considers sticking on a butterfly bandage, but it would only get caught up in her hair. Decides to let it scab over. He holds a gauze pad to it, presses lightly.

"You're sweet," Grace murmurs. Her eyes flicker, seem to roll a bit, unfocused. She shuts them.

"You're going to have a headache," he says. Carter does not mention his fears about a possible concussion. Her eyes don't look right. *What do they say about concussions?* He tries to remember. *If she falls asleep, does she die?*

Am I supposed to keep her from sleeping?

Is that a real thing or a TV thing?

He simply doesn't know.

Add it to the list.

He probes Grace's side.

"Ow," she says. "Stop."

"You're warm," he tells her. "I don't know if there's anything we can do about your ribs. We don't have a lot of wrap, and we should probably save it for your ankle. How's your breathing?"

Grace tries to take a deep breath. "It hurts," she admits. "Stabbing pain. Like a knife digging into me."

"Okay, then. Probably best if you don't breathe," Carter advises.

Grace smirks. "Don't breathe, got it."

Her arms and legs are banged and bruised. Nothing seems to be broken. He uses handfuls of water from the canteen to rinse the scratches clean. There's a deep, ugly gash on her right calf. The flesh is badly torn, like a hunk of meat has been bitten out of it by a shark. Carter makes a face. Normally this stuff grosses him out. But there's no time for feeling queasy. He digs into the kit and pulls out the hydrogen peroxide. Shakes it, says, "If I remember correctly, this is going to sting."

Without further warning, he pours the peroxide directly into the wound. Grace's leg reflexively stiffens; she finds and squeezes his hand; white bubbles rise and pop. Carter does his best patching it up, using a combination of gauze pads and butterfly strips. It's not a work of art. He dreads dealing with her ankle. Feels sure it's broken or shattered. "Do you want to try to sit up?" he asks.

Grace slowly lifts herself up on her elbows. She blows out air from her mouth in audible gusts. "This position . . . sucks," she says, and lies back down again, defeated.

"Maybe," he says softly and soothingly, "you can scooch back. You could try sitting up and resting against the rock wall." He notices there's a slight overhang, providing shade. Carter goes to her backpack, digs out her flannel shirt for a pillow. Unfolding the shirt, he discovers the energy bars she has stashed away.

"What's this?" he asks.

Grace smiles. "I was saving them for your birthday. Have one."

Carter feels he should be angry with her, but he's too happy about the thought of food. He tears open the wrapper, breaks the bar in two, offers half to Grace. She shakes her head. "Not now."

Sitka comes by his side, eyes fixed on the food, leaning in. It's not like her to beg. He breaks off a smaller chuck, holds it in his open palm. The dog gobbles it down. Carter does the same. He zips the four remaining bars in the backpack. Makes a mental note to carefully go through both packs, make an accounting of what they've got.

"Can you stand?" he asks.

Grace shakes her head.

"Maybe if you sit up," he says, a little more forcefully. "It might make you feel better. I'll help."

He leans over and awkwardly helps Grace come to a sitting

position. She stifles a cry of pain, counts out a series of short breaths. The wall is ten feet behind her.

"Can you just . . . ?"

Grace turns her head to check the distance and makes a decision. Pushing with her left foot, leaving the right extended, she backward drags herself to the wall. The effort exhausts her. "I'll take that Advil," she says.

Carter ignores her request.

"Carter," she repeats.

"Let's wait," he answers. "Just to be careful. Like you said."

She's too tired to fight. He gets her as comfortable as possible, propping her up with the backpacks and shirt.

Next Carter moves down to her feet. He tenderly unlaces both boots, spreads them as wide as possible. "I'm going to take them off," he informs the patient.

Grace nods.

He starts with the left boot. It slips off effortlessly. He pulls off Grace's sock, wipes her bare foot with his hands. She wiggles her toes. His hands move to the right foot.

"Wait," she says.

He waits. One hand below the heel, the other by the toe.

"Okay," she says.

He tugs, ever so gently. Wiggles it, pulls more. The boot doesn't budge.

"Easy," she scolds.

He leans back, sweat sticking to the back of his shirt, and looks at her. "I have to, Grace," he whispers. "I'm sorry."

He yanks off the boot.

She screams, tears pour out of her eyes. She curses and

fumes. After a time, he slowly unpeels her sock. The ankle is ridiculously swollen, twice its normal size, three times the size. It is puffy from the top of her foot, all around the back, up to the knobs of her ankle. The coloration is red with early signs of black and blue. Carter sits crisscross, softly places the foot in his lap, touches it with the tips of his fingers. He's aware of his own limitations, but for Grace's sake pretends that he has an idea what he's doing.

He settles for kindness. "Poor Grace," he says.

Sitka smells deeply, her whiskers brushing against Grace's skin. The dog licks at her legs, the blood and sweat, working intently. Grace tilts her head back against the wall, eyes closed. "I messed up, Cart. I really screwed this up."

"Shhh," her brother answers. "Just rest."

After a long silence, he stirs. Places her bare foot on the ground. When that doesn't work—"Hell to the no!" she declares—he tucks a backpack below her knee, raising the ankle off the ground. "I need to find water," he informs Grace.

She nods in agreement, eyes closed.

"I'll be right back," he says. "Don't go running off on me."

Grace smiles. "I was thinking of joining the circus."

Carter assesses the landscape. Behind them, there is a rock wall. Grace landed on a fairly level surface, rock slabs and dirt and green ground cover form a rough flatness. It will do for now. From here, facing forward, the land slopes gently downward in all directions. Trees randomly everywhere, sparse at first but more densely packed together farther down the slope. There's something forbidding about it, even in this afternoon daylight, an impenetrable quality. The deep, dark wood. He decides to search for water methodically in widening semicircles, ranging from left to right, then back again.

For once, he gets lucky.

To the right, just thirty yards away, he notices a shimmering rock. Moving closer, he realizes it is damp. On his hands and knees, he explores the tall grasses and small yellow wildflowers and mossy ground with his hands. It is moist, soggy even. He looks up, back the way Grace fell. As if reading the mountain, he imagines the path where excess runoff from hard rains might trickle down the hillside. He stands, searching the ground with his eyes, shifts to his right, and it appears: a shallow depression of water on slabs of sedimentary rock, less than nine inches deep, fed by a trickle, as if pausing there before drifting down at gravity's request.

"Yes!" he says, shaking a fist like a golfer who's just birdied a long putt.

Carter hustles back and refills both water bottles. He drinks one—thirstier than he realized—hearing the loud gulp and slosh of water hitting an empty stomach. He hands a bottle to Grace.

"You did good, Cart," she says.

He nods, grateful to hear it.

"Do you think it's safe?" Grace asks.

Carter hadn't considered that. "I hope so," he answers. "I just drank a bottle of it." Right now, dirty water is the least of their problems.

[A PLAN]

As dusk approaches, Grace and Carter must face another night on the mountain. At least it's not raining. The air is dry and warm. They need a plan.

Carter suggests, "First thing in the morning, I'll go for help."

"No, you won't," Grace sharply protests. "No splitting up. It's dangerous. I won't let you."

Carter keeps his thoughts to himself. He goes with Sitka into the timber to search for something that could serve as a walking stick. He finds a long branch that should work. He carries it back to Grace. Sitka lies back down, head between her paws, and watches them. "Let's test your ankle. We need to see if you can walk." He hands the stick to her. "Try using this as a crutch."

Grace frowns. She hasn't moved for the past several hours. Her ankle has ballooned to the size of a melon. It is already turning blue and purple. Her head throbs; her body aches. It feels like she's been run over by a bus.

"If you can't even do this, Grace, how are we going to walk out of here? I can't carry you."

"You aren't going alone," Grace insists. "It's too dangerous."

"You don't think I can do it?" he asks.

Grace's lips tighten. She looks away, holds out a hand. "Pull me up."

Carter clasps her with two hands, leans back, knees bent,

and pulls. Grace springs to her feet, hops once, twice, holding her injured foot off the ground. Nausea surges through her in woozy waves, shrouds her vision. She grimaces, steadies herself with the stick. Staring straight ahead, she's determined not to throw up, her eyes fixed on the trunk of a big oak. An acidic taste of bile fills the back of her throat.

Carter watches, fearful she might collapse. His sister's face is ashen, pale. Her injured leg is bent, foot dangling uselessly behind her. Even standing is too much for her right now. Still, she is stubborn by nature, and he needs to prove a point. "Can you put any weight on it?" he asks.

Grace tentatively touches the ball of her right foot to the ground. An involuntary groan comes from deep inside her body, the foot instantly lifts off the ground. "I can't," she confesses. "Maybe tomorrow."

Carter shakes his head. This isn't good.

"Cart, I really need to pee," Grace says.

He doesn't understand at first.

"Do you mind?" she says, making a semicircle with her down-turned index finger.

She wants him to turn around. "Wait, here?" he asks.

Grace hops over a few feet. She's not happy about it, either, but it's the best she can do.

When she's done, Carter covers the puddle with handfuls of dirt and leaves. He helps Grace get back into a sitting position. Even the effort to accomplish that task—the simple act of sitting down—takes its toll. She stares off, taking shallow breaths, waiting for the pain to subside.

"I'm sorry," she says, her voice small.

He looks at her, nods. Doesn't know what to say.

Twilight is gathering, the darkness filling in the edges of the timber. It gives the impression that the forest is creeping closer. Like a living creature, crowding them. He picks up the water bottles. "Come, Sitka." The dog follows the boy to the narrow stream. Carter refreshes both bottles. Sitka steps in to drink.

"I forbid you to go," Grace calls down after him.

He looks up at her, doesn't reply.

"I mean it, Cart."

He doesn't bother to argue. There's no point. The time for talking is over. She'll never agree.

[QUEST]

He decides during the fitful night while listening to Grace suffer in the dark. Moans and murmurs and garbled words, each sound riding on a wave of fear. In sleep, Grace's confident front drops away like a mask. His brave sister's vulnerability is revealed, hurt and frightened and needing help. He can't wait for her approval. She is in no position to decide. The track star has passed the baton to her little brother, only she doesn't yet realize it.

The fall has changed everything.

It's up to him now.

Carter understands they'll never make it out of there together. They have no food, no real survival skills. More crucial, Grace might need medical attention, and soon. Getting help is their best hope. So at the first glimmer of light, Carter heads out, carrying a near-empty backpack and a full bottle of water. He leaves the rest of the supplies, meager as they are, for Grace. The emergency blanket, the first aid kit, the flashlight, the knife, her flannel, a full bottle of water. He takes one energy bar for his travels and leaves the last three for Grace.

Sitka hurries after the boy as he starts up the slope. The faithful dog follows, tail swishing, perhaps eager to explore together. Maybe just curious to know what's going on. Sitka pushes to the lead.

"No," Carter commands in a harsh whisper. "You stay, guard Grace."

The dog steps toward the boy again. Searches his face for information, for guidance, for reassurance. Receives only a cold stare.

"No," Carter repeats, voice still soft. He doesn't want to wake his sister.

The dog persists. Sitka jumps, pivots on her rear legs, makes a beeline back down the path toward Grace. Turns again, watching; comes back to Carter, repeats the pantomime. Sitka wants the boy to rejoin to Grace. The pack, together.

Carter picks up a rock, holds it behind his right ear. "I said no," he threatens, voice trembling.

Could Sitka smell it, the boy's raw emotion? Could the dog perceive the shimmering wetness in Carter's eyes? One way or another, Sitka gets the message. She lowers her tail between her legs, ears pinned back, gaze to the ground. Slinks away.

Carter turns his back on the dog, and on his sister, and picks a path up the slope. He plans to make it to the high crest. And from there . . . he'll see what he can see. They made it this far. He just has to find the way back.

His hike has become a journey; his journey, a quest.

Carter has one simple goal.

He only needs to save their lives.

[HUNTRESS]

Sitka nudges the sleeping girl. Pushes her nose into Grace's armpit, senses the girl's deep discomfort. The boy, gone. Something amiss. Nudges more forcefully.

Grace stirs, rolls to her side on the hard surface, winces, face knotted in pain. She eases back, reaches a hand sleepily out in the direction of the dog, sleeps again.

After a time, the dog moves away, climbs down off the rock face, down into the sun-stippled understory beneath the great shade-cooled umbrella of leaves. A hunger gnaws at Sitka's belly like a twisting, tightening coil of wire. Imagine if everything a human sees—every color, shape, and texture—arrived with a specific odor. The red of that flower's petals, the deep-rutted bark of a poplar, the light brown of a wren's chest, the dropped acorns, the pale underside of a leaf, the shimmering sky itself: every pixel that an eye apprehends, for a dog those details come with a singular odor, as different as green from red, blue from yellow. When Sitka sniffs, it is the same as Grace opening her eyes. Sitka inhales and her tail sweeps and she knows a man has passed near here some time ago, moving in an easterly direction. A mosaic of smells, each one a discovery. The creatures of this world announce themselves to her nose: *I am.* The dog goes to the slow-trickling stream. Movement among the ferns. Sitka stealthily moves to investigate, prodded by the ache in her belly. Plunges her nose deep into the living green world, inhales the data points, sniffs out the whiskered, stout rodent. Pounces with front paws outstretched, and again—there! success!—bites down, gulps, gone.

A huntress!

Sweet vole!

And even in that instant, the dog attends to one who lies restless in half sleep; a soft moan, she wakes. Meal in belly—hair and tail and skull—Sitka will be at Grace's side by the time she opens her eyes.

[PEACE]

Makayla doesn't feel up to cooking this morning. She splashes her face with cold water, gets dressed, and drives twenty minutes into town for a much-deserved treat. Her mind is on a hot stack of blueberry pancakes. Glass of OJ. The daily paper. She's curious to read how the escaped mountain lion—not to mention the grotesque mauling—is playing in the local media. She enjoys the solitude of her rustic cabin, but sometimes Makayla misses the clank of coffee cups and cutlery on classic American white-laminate tabletops, the low buzz of talk punctuated by eruptions of laughter from the regulars at Sally's Restaurant. Today is one of those days. She misses human companionship. For Makayla, a little bit goes a long way.

A call comes in as she turns onto Main Street.

"Hey, Brooklyn, got a job for you," Lieutenant Frank Watkins says.

Makayla is surprised. Usually she works independently. The calls that do come through are almost always from dispatch. This feels different. She picks up on her lieutenant's urgency right away. Not his usual joking preamble. He's down to business. "Yes, sir?" she asks.

"A couple of day hikers found a heart attack victim on Blood Mountain about half an hour ago. Heavyset guy, midfifties, best guess, looks like he collapsed out there," Frank explains.

A dozen questions leap into Makayla's mind. "Alive?" she asks.

"Touch and go," Frank says. "They found him about ten feet off the trail. Called nine-one-one, who in turn reached out to DEC Central. We extracted him via hoist operation. The helicopter transported him to County General."

Makayla says, "You could have called me sooner."

Frank replies, "Yeah, well, you've been putting in a lot of hours. Figured you might need your rest."

Makayla asks, "How long was he out there?"

Frank says, "Well, I'm hoping you can help us figure that out. Right now we've got more questions than answers. Looks like he had a heart attack, probably while off-trail watering a tree. Took a big bump to the head. Seems they found him when he was in the process of crawling back. Pretty bad shape. Rained on, bitten by insects, clothes damp and covered in mud."

"Must be a hard guy," she says. "Not many heart attacks make it off the mountain."

"That's true," Frank says. "When they reached him, they say he lifted two fingers like a peace sign, rolled over, and passed out."

"A peace sign? Some old hippie?" Makayla muses. "He was alone? You contact the family yet?"

"Not so simple," Frank replies. "Haven't made a positive ID. Guy had nothing in his pockets. No wallet, not a thing. You know how it is—these hikers don't want to risk losing their American Express card in the woods. His backpack had a sweatshirt, compass, water bottle, three peanut butter and jelly sandwiches. Plus safety matches in a waterproof case."

Makayla eases down on the brake, puts the big red Ford into park. "I just pulled up to Sally's. I'm going to grab an egg sandwich to go. I'll drive over to the trailhead. I assume this guy left a car in the parking lot."

Franks says, "They didn't find keys among his effects."

Makayla thought that over. She'd have a look-see for herself. "Well, he got to the trailhead somehow. I doubt he rode in on a moose. Let me order my breakfast, Frank. I'll catch you up later."

"How long?" he asks.

"Forty minutes if I hurry," Makayla replies. "And I'll be hurrying. I'll let you know what I find out."

"Listen, Brooklyn. I would have asked the search-and-rescue team to do it, but they were a little preoccupied with saving this man's life. Make sure you review the trail registry. See if this guy filled out an itinerary. Maybe he wasn't alone—you know what I'm saying."

It was a new thought. Makayla pondered it. Possible, she decided. Heart attack off the trail. Overweight male in his fifties. Likely a slow hiker. Maybe his fellow hikers took off ahead of him. A classic mistake. Hikers of mixed abilities often get separated in the wilderness. It can lead to serious problems. But why wouldn't they call it in after they discovered he was missing? It didn't add up.

No, she thought. *Almost definitely alone.*

[GONE]

Even before she fully wakes, Grace knows.

She knows it in her bones.

He's gone.

And it scares her. Not for being abandoned. But the thought of Carter wandering off on his own frightens her to the core. She pictures his soft cheeks, long eyelashes, and skinny body. He hasn't even started middle school yet. Her little brother wants so badly to be the hero.

Without another thought, she cries out in her loudest voice, "Carter!" It burns her chest. Her voice does not echo back. Instead, it is swallowed by the wildness, absorbed by the trees. No answer. She is alone.

Yet in the wake of her cry, new sounds reach Grace's ears. Birds in the trees, singing their songs; fat wrens hopping on the ground, pecking for bugs, worms, grubs. Scissor-tailed warblers swooping low, darting from branch to branch. Busy with their unfathomable lives. Grace listens to their music as they chatter back and forth. It reminds her of a recent family vacation, trying to follow the conversations in a Quebec restaurant. *What are you saying?* She tries to guess.

And Grace decides it's this:

Good morning, good morning, good morning to you!

Roused by the birds, Grace pulls herself up to sitting position.

Like a bedside nurse, Sitka watches the girl intently. Grace runs her tongue across her teeth, wishes for mint toothpaste. She polishes her teeth with the top of her shirt. She examines the scrapes, cuts, and bruises along her body. Breathing is still painful. Best to move slowly, deliberately. *Is her darkened ankle actually larger? It has ballooned up to the size of . . . a balloon?* Grace laughs at her little joke, a snort through the nose.

Her hips and ribs ache. Her ankle actually feels okay, so long as she doesn't put any pressure on it. What an awful night's sleep. Grace reaches for the backpack, pulls it close. She finds the Advil bottle, rinses down three tablets with water. Her heart sinks when she sees that Carter has left three energy bars, the Mylar emergency blanket, her flannel, the spare socks, the medical kit, and the knife. He took only one energy bar, his extra shirt, and a water bottle. Hopefully he snagged the moleskin for his blisters.

The dressing for the deep gash in her leg had peeled off in the night. Grace tentatively pokes at the wound. The skin appears inflamed. She fears infection. Hard to keep anything clean out here. Grace treats it again with peroxide. It doesn't seem to help. The edges of the gash are turning black. Not cool. She rolls the gauze around her calf, holds it in place with a piece of duct tape. All she feels in that spot is a pulsing throb, as if her heart had migrated to a new part of her body. The blood pumping: *ba-thrum, ba-thrum, ba-thrum.*

This activity causes Grace to grow dizzy. A headache behind her brow announces itself and reverberates like a symphony's clanged cymbal. She feels instantly nauseous. Shuts her eyes from the light, waits. Suddenly she pitches to the side, retches convulsively with little in her stomach. Grace gags and dry-heaves. As her stomach muscles contract, the stabbing sensation at her side returns, like a blunt knife twisting into her rib cage. Grace finally spits, wipes her mouth. "Ohhhh," she groans, miserably. "Mama."

And still the birds make music.

Agitated and upset, Sitka steps away to venture into the near woods.

I'm alive, Grace reminds herself. *It's not nothing.*

Her mind drifts to her mama, the bravest person Grace knows. And her best friend. Each year, Grace's mother's condition gradually worsens. Her body grows weaker; her muscles atrophy. Multiple sclerosis has taken away so much, left her confined to a wheelchair, limited her in so many ways, yet Grace has never once heard her mother complain. Instead, she smiles her dimpled smile, manages to bake something elaborate and delicious every weekend, diligently goes through her exercise routine each morning, and cruises all over creation in her motorized wheelchair. Unstoppable.

Grace decides to rest for a while. Take a breather. The headache will pass. Later she'll need to refill the water bottle. That should be fun.

[ON THE RIM]

Carter's day begins with purpose and determination. And more than that, for Carter: a sense of freedom and a chance to prove himself. So much depends on him. The air is hot and soupy. He finds a trickling streambed and gulps handfuls of cool, clear water. Tops off his water bottle; sets his hat backward. The sun's up there lost in the hazy, overcast sky, but he doesn't think to locate it.

He makes his way to the ridge's rim where Grace first tumbled. From the vantage point of his ascent, Carter can easily recognize how it was a false summit. Not nearly to the top, so much still obscured. The limited view provides him with no answers. He dumbly stares out at the simmering countryside. Carter can almost imagine wiggly lines of heat, like in cartoon drawings, rising from the treetops to the sky. He feels a shuddering thrill to be alone in this place, hundreds of empty miles radiating out in all directions. Big peaks here and there. Valleys below. Ridges across. No roads, no cabins, no signs of human activity. Carter is not disappointed. He expected this. He remembered Grace's initial reaction, the discouraged look on her face before she went down. For a moment there, watching her fall, he thought she had died.

Carter pauses to chew the last bite of his energy bar. He needs to keep going. Get to an even higher spot where he can get the best possible overview, pick a direction, and stick to it. Still he lingers.

Two hawks ride wind currents, surfers in the sky, the tips of their wings making microadjustments. Carter needs to remember this spot. There's no point going for help if he can't lead them back to Grace. He cannot fail. It all looks like an undifferentiated mass of leaves to him. He notes a sheer rock face across the way, the conical summit of a high peak, the expanse of wide valley below. A group of white tree trunks—aspen? birch?—the words are vaguely familiar. He builds a cairn, something he's seen before, though he does not know the word. It is a small pile of rough stones. Obviously man-made. He tucks the bar wrapper under the top rock, a little flash of yellow to catch someone's eye. Along the ridge to his right, he spies three deer grazing farther along the rim. He could target them with a well-thrown stone. One deer lifts its head, turns to regard him. Carter does not move. Just watches. The deer turn and ride off on spindly, brown legs. A mother and two fawns.

[CLUES]

There are five vehicles parked in the woodland lot, including Makayla's truck. This is the head of the trail, the starting point to the peak of Blood Mountain, eventually back down to Crater Lake, and any other of about twelve different, increasingly far-flung destinations. All in all, not the most popular spot in parkland. Hard to get to, mostly. Not a high-profile summit. The park is a vast, interconnected web of trails, spurs, and dead ends. In the spaces between and outside that network of trails—the peaks, ponds, bogs, pastures, and lean-tos—there remain dense, secluded areas that only the most austere backcountry hikers have ever laid eyes upon. Makayla thinks of it this way: *Land as it used to be.* Still a few places in this country that have been left unspoiled. It's a sprawling park, and some parts are as wild as the cry in a wolf's throat.

Most hikers are pretty responsible about filling in the registry. Time of arrival, number in party, destination, day hike or overnight, that kind of thing. If somebody's lost, this information provides the first, best clue as to where they were headed. It gives the search focus and saves valuable time. Otherwise the search-and-rescue team is just throwing darts in the darkness. In those cases it becomes, once reason overtakes hope, a search-and-*recover* team, faced with the unholy task of filling a body bag and carrying it down the mountain. Hopefully it won't come to that.

Without a name to match to the book, it's guesswork for Makayla to accurately know who's who. She runs her finger down the columns, sees nothing but day hikers for the past week. Three of them today. Six yesterday. She turns to contemplate the parked cars. One of them, she's 98 percent certain, is the victim's. She walks over, thinking how it rained pretty hard two nights ago. Ground still damp in lower depressions where there would have been puddles just yesterday. Only one car has a damp leaf still stuck to the front windshield wiper. Makayla lowers to her hands and knees, studies the ground. She reaches under a yellow Volvo and feels the dirt. Bone-dry. Bingo. This car, she figures, has been here since before the rain.

She rises, wipes her hands against her pants. Makayla leans against the window, peers inside. Big car for one guy. Why would one man, traveling alone, drive such a big car? The driver's seat is pushed way back, which adds up. They said he was about 250 pounds. On the back seat, there's a blanket and a candy wrapper. She sees an open paperback, spine up. The cover features a picture of a red dragon. Teen fantasy. It worries her.

It worries her a lot.

The doors are locked.

Standard procedure says it's time to pass this over to the state police. Makayla thinks about the possibility of two hikers lost up there on the mountain. A driver, and someone in the front passenger seat, and someone else—almost surely a teen or tween—in the back. Three people total. Did she have probable cause to search the vehicle?

Makayla steps back, slowly circles the car. She spies a flat rock that's out of place, just inside the driver's front wheel. She reaches down, lifts the rock, and lo: one set of car keys. Makayla smiles to herself. It's good to be queen. She recalls a phrase she's heard before: "Ask forgiveness, not permission." Better to act now and risk breaking a rule than to wait and lose valuable time. She presses the key fob, and the lock springs open.

She pops open the glove compartment. It's jammed with registration papers, old maps, work gloves, a tire gauge, some sort of silver cylinder—Makayla realizes it's a whistle—and a screwdriver. Beneath it all, she finds a wallet and a cell phone. Yeah, this is the guy. He's from downstate. David Taylor. Access to the phone is blocked, needs a fingerprint to open it. Damn technology. There's another phone in the side pocket of the front passenger door. Dead batteries. Cell phones start roaming for a signal out here and it kills the battery, real quick. Nothing's easy. She reaches back and picks up the paperback, flips it open to the inside front cover. There's a name printed in what appears to be a young person's handwriting: CARTER TAYLOR, MS. TURO.

Another thing: the car smells like dog. Sure enough, there's hair on the back seat. Black and gray, medium length. Shepherd, maybe. She flips down the visor for the front passenger seat. Down drops a pair of cheap sunglasses. Kind of funky, though. Judging by the shape and style, almost definitely a girl's. "Not good" just got worse. Now she's thinking: *two kids*.

Makayla remembers the three sandwiches in the father's backpack. He was carrying food for all of them. He had the waterproof matches, too. And the map. She recalls the detail from his discovery, how he flashed his rescuers a peace sign. Two fingers. Maybe he was trying to say something else. Two more, up on the mountain.

They haven't come down yet.

Time to call dispatch. A lot of wheels will start turning. Makayla needs to stay rooted to the scene until she can pass it over to the next ranger in charge. More will trickle in. They'll organize a command post, possibly at the volunteer fire department in town. Maybe bring in the van to establish a mobile command post here. Call in the volunteers, start marking up the grid maps, coordinate the search. It won't be until tomorrow morning when they're fully operational. Makayla looks up at the sky, checks the height of the sun, studies the clouds. She aches to get up that mountain, start running trails. Thinks: *If those kids have been out there more than twenty-four hours, the dogs won't be any use at all. The trail's gone cold.*

[WAY-FINDER]

Carter pushes himself too hard on the ascent and now pays the toll. The hike leaves him hunched over, hands on his knees, gasping for oxygen. Two nights on the hard ground and three days without proper nutrition have left him drained, near empty. He shakes his head, mind sputtering.

He slugs down water. Waits.

His heartbeat slowly regulates.

Carter rises and looks around. The view opens up: wider, farther, more expansive. He spots a lake an incalculable distance away. It looks far, but doable. From these heights, it's hard to tell. He holds out an arm and traces the pathway: go down and bend around, then straightaway. Is that *his* lake? Crater Lake? Where they were supposed to go? He can't know for sure. Carter's brain struggles to perform an impossible task—to form a mental map of the route from the car. He wants to rediscover the trail. *How did we get here?* In his fantasy, he yearns to stand on his tippy-toes to see his father impatiently waiting by the car down below. Imagine that.

To his right, one tree stands in the forefront, like a proud sentinel, taller than the rest. More elegant, more perfectly proportioned. Almost as if it doesn't belong. A lone survivor from a stricken tribe. The tree takes the general shape of an umbrella, with wide-spreading limbs and a few low-dropping branches that seem to wave at him in greeting. *Come, Carter,* the tree says, *I know the way.*

Carter is surprised.

The way-finder knows his name.

Carter walks, limping slightly from blisters on his right foot, to the great tree. The gray-green bark at its wide base is furrowed with deep grooves. His head tilts back in wonder. Must be fifty feet tall, a hundred years old, maybe more. Somehow he senses, like never before, that he is in the presence of an ancient, mysterious, living creature. An alive thing. *Hey, Tree.* His right hand reaches up, fingertips almost touch the lowest branch. Carter impulsively jumps, catches hold, swings his legs, hoists himself up.

He begins to climb.

Rises branch by branch.

He exhilarates in the texture of the rough bark in his hands. His arms straining, reaching; his back muscles heaving. Timbers creak and groan, and still he climbs. He comes to a spot where two branches split off and upward, forming a V shape. Carter finds that he can lean against the trunk, his feet propped against each limb, and comfortably relax. He's a lookout in the crow's nest, a pirate's skull-and-crossbones flag blowing in the breeze, searching the riotous green sea. *Shiver me timbers!*

The view stuns him. The land is laid out like a map draped across an uneven table. Off in the distance, beyond what he accepts to be Crater Lake, he discerns a dirt road needled through the wilderness like a faint thread. So far away, but at last a lodestar for his wanderings.

I am not lost, he thinks.

I am right here.

This is the gift he receives from the tree.

A small, low-flying plane angles past. Carter waves uselessly. No one can see him. Carter's attention turns to the tree itself. The leaves are oval with saw-toothed edges and silver-green undersides. A bug inches along a limb. Carter wonders if it has ever touched the ground. Its entire life spent in this aerial wonderland. A wind sweeps across the valley. The wide canopy moves; debris patters down. The upper trunk, the great ship's mast, sways in the swells. Carter is not afraid. He feels as if he is nestled safely inside a lost kingdom, a palace of secrets. *Does the tree know I'm here?*

It is a fine place to think. But Carter knows it is time to move. He imagines the route as if it were as simple as going around the block to buy milk. He'll descend into the valley, then circle around and to the right, then straightaway to reach the lake. Piece of cake. There will be people there. A man fishing. A young family camping, children swimming in the water, laughing. Eating s'mores.

His stomach churns. He remembers food.

Hold on, Grace, he thinks.

Carter climbs down, swings from the lowest branch, drops soundlessly to the earth.

[TRACKS]

I t is not his nature to speak. The angular man is like a solitary fir with roots in soil, branches reaching to the sun. There are no words for this. It is enough to be, to stand, to watch, to sleep. Once he came upon a lone hiker, gave a terse nod, uttered a hoarse *Hey*, and never broke stride. His throat dry, his voice a rasp. On night raids, he moves around the outskirts of town like a furtive fox in the dusky, slate-gray meadow. On the rare times he ventures into town, for bulk items at the food co-op or essentials at Walmart, he washes his hands, files his fingernails, trims his beard. He shrinks himself, becomes anonymous. He selects his supplies, avoids eye contact, pays in cash, and vanishes.

He still thinks in words, of course. But less and less. The angular man knows the names of things: hickory, sweetleaf, black cherry, chestnut. Which mushrooms he can eat, which to avoid. On and on with the names of things. But he no longer feels compelled to make those noises with his mouth. For why? For whom? For what purpose?

Simpler, and safer, this way.

He once lived in a world of words and commands and roadside bombs and snipers and death. A world of IEDs buried underground, "improvised explosive devices," a nine-syllable way of saying "homemade bombs." Where a false step—no, not false— just a step, an unfortunate footfall, a *true* step—and the whole world explodes. Bodies tossed into the air like confetti. The boot is gone. The foot, the leg up to the knee, the soft undersides of the groin, and then the screaming starts, cries of "Help me!" and "Oh my God!" and "Morphine, morphine!"

Always the shouting. Everything said in exclamation points. But it was the sounds *before* words that haunt him. How when you are hit—a sniper bullet to the shoulder from a Russian-built, semiautomatic rifle nearly half a mile away—the body makes a cracking noise, and it is the body that talks first. Sounds that can't be typed or imitated or unheard. A river of gurgling blood.

He recalls feeling relieved that it wasn't his turn yet.

The wood helps silence those sounds, and replaces them with new wonders—the natural world.

Peace and quietude.

Most days, anyway.

The man of the forest stops in his tracks, drops to his haunches to stare at a print in the mud. He lightly touches it with his fingertips, measures the size against his own hand. He notes the distinctive M-shaped pad pattern, with three lobes on the rear of the heel. *Could he be mistaken?* It is easy to confuse dog tracks for lion tracks. They are incredibly similar. He checks for claw marks—cats rarely show claw marks in their track—the toe position, and the overall shape of the heel pad. Finally, he's sure. His head lifts, scans the underbrush for signs. A tangle of sumacs, black locust, buckthorn. He listens to the activities all around him: the trills of songbirds, the calls of the crickets, the chitchatting of chipmunks. The print puzzles him. A cat? Here? He's never seen signs of mountain lions in this region before.

The idea unsettles him.

Lions are furtive killers.

The expression he heard from a father he once knew: "If you see a mountain lion, son, it is already too late."

He thinks of the boy, traveling alone. Surely headed into a world of hurt. Bogland.

[BOG]

There is no discernible trail. To Carter, it is simple: he is *here* and wishes to be *there*. So he opts to bomb straight down like a daredevil at a ski resort. Seems faster that way, but it isn't. He bushwhacks through rough terrain, stumbling on rocks and roots, getting tangled up in prickly thickets. The downward movement is tough on his joints. His toes jam into the front of his boots, blisters form on the bottoms of his feet. With each painful step, Carter grows more distressed. Fresh fears about Grace push into his consciousness; he feels guilty about leaving her behind. *What if this is another mistake?* He misses Sitka's calming presence. Feels so alone. After a brief rest to regroup, Carter determinedly blunders downhill—only to later realize he's forgotten his water bottle. Carter pictures it in his mind, exactly where he set it down. He can't face the thought of going back uphill for it, so he stumbles forward, blind and bottleless.

He sneezes and puts on his second shirt; it makes no difference. Plowing forward, Carter takes a hard hit from an overhanging branch. The blow staggers him, knocks him to his knees. He stays on all fours, woozy. He touches his head, his fingers are wet and red. He sits back, resting on one arm, dazed, holding the shirt-sleeve of his outer wrist against the wound. The shirt becomes wet with blood. Streaks trickle down the left side of his face. He gathers himself, continues the descent. He trips on roots, skids on slick surfaces, and falls against jagged rocks, slicing his fingers. Carter finds that his legs no longer work properly. A bloody gash forms on his left knee, bleeding into his boot. Each blow, each misstep drains something vital out of him. Slowly his energy leaks away, deflated like a forgotten birthday balloon.

Despite all this, Carter remains determined to plunge forward. He walks unquestioningly into a wall of dense vegetation. The summer tangle of branches grope like sinister arms. Hellish snags claw at his flesh, rip his shirt. Carter fails to recognize that he is headed into acidic bogland. Plants do not thrive here. Trees suffer from the lack of nutrients. The bog smells foul, of rot and dank decay. His mind is a lawn mower that won't start. It sputters and fails to catch.

The boy keeps going. Traveling blind, he feels drugged, exhausted. He steps into mud, slips again, falls. His eyes shut for an instant, and he doesn't remember falling asleep. A droning chorus of insects wakes him. His eyes widen, he pitches forward, panicked, and sinks into three inches of murky, muddy water. The ground wants to swallow him whole. He grabs his leg by the knee and yanks it from the sucking earth. His boot comes back black. Both of his feet are soaked to the skin.

Carter keeps fighting, keeps moving forward.

Bog all around him.

He longs for firm footing, a drying fire.

Twilight drops down like a quivering leaf. The bugs gather in swarms. For the first half hour, Carter slaps at them, waves his hands, rubs his arms and legs, scratches furiously, even howls out loud; mosquitoes, gorged with his blood, explode when slapped on his forearms and legs. Reinforcements come to take their place. In desperation, Carter smears black ooze all over his skin and face, gets it in his mouth and ears. Eventually, he surrenders. His tender face reduced to a swollen welt, blistered and raw. Black flies take turns tormenting him. They dive and bite and veer away. His eyelids swell, his left eye nearly shut.

He weaves, falls, despairs, rises again.

He cannot stop here.

He cannot die.

Carter Taylor is eleven years old, and he feels his life wavering on some great precipice.

Grace, his feverish mind recalls.

In the relative openness of the bog, he easily sees the stars in the velvet sky. *When did it become night? When in the world have there ever been so many pinpricks of light?*

He feels cold to the core.

Shivering, wet, bone-tired.

He keeps walking, staggering, reeling through the reeds, bumping into dead, bare, nutrient-starved trees.

His boots fill with water. White wormlike bugs discover his flesh. Carter can't seem to compel his feet to move. He finds himself leaning against a dead tree. He pauses to rest for a moment, a minute, an hour. He doesn't remember. His mind blank, a void. Fear slaps him awake. Instinct yanks at his collar, shakes him. If he stays in this grievous bog, he won't live to see the morning. It is the one clear thought in his muddled mind. Can't stay here.

The temperature drops.

He blunders into the black.

He steps and his foot does not sink.

Another step. The ground holds.

Another, and another.

Carter hangs his head, drops to his knees, begins to crawl, feels the firm earth under his hands.

He's made it through.

So tired, so tired.

Carter stumbles another seventy-five yards, losing his hat in the process. He collapses, curls into a ball beneath a weeping willow that has taken root in the rot. He does not wonder at the way the graceful giant's branches sweep downward, or how its long, slender leaves resemble tears of tree sorrow and tree remorse. *How did it come to grow so sad?* He does not wonder at all. Just knows in his bones. The cold presses against him. He shivers in anguish. His body begins to shake convulsively. He rolls and looks to the sky.

I am not lost, he thinks. *The world is lost.*

I am right here. I am right here. And there is the moon, right where it is supposed to be.

[SEEKING]

Walking has always been the engine for Makayla's deepest thoughts. All her adult life, she's happiest out on the trail. It gives a body time to think. Her thought is focused like a laser on those two lost children. She knows their names and ages now, since the DEC has been able to contact their mother: Grace, thirteen, and Carter, eleven. Plus the dog, a mutt named Sitka.

The weather report is suboptimal. More fog tonight. Not unusual around here this time of year—moisture carried by the nearby lakes, the cooling land meets a warm front. Plus something about the dew point. Makayla isn't the world's greatest meteorologist. Not her strong suit. The lowered visibility should be just enough to make her job impossible. Might be best to rest up and hit this full force in the morning.

Every once in a while she pauses, cups her hands around her mouth, calls out, "Grace! Carter!" She listens. Raises her binoculars, glasses the terrain. Keeps moving. In fog, when water molecules have a dampening effect on sound, Makayla knows that low-pitched notes travel best. It is why foghorns on the water use that low-pitched, haunting moan.

There won't be large search parties out past dusk. Barely time to get organized. The escaped "man-killer" lion—as the media tells it—has siphoned off some resources. But you do the best you can. Makayla walks and focuses on the trail. She asks herself: *How do people get lost? What mistakes do they make?* If Makayla can think like those kids, turned-around and lost in unknown parkland, maybe it will help her find them.

It's easy enough to stray off the trail. Head down, maybe moving too quickly, eager to get there, not vigilant enough for markers. Everyone does it, even the most experienced hikers. But then you figure it out. The smart ones backtrack. She remembers something an instructor once told her during training: *We have eyes in front of our head*. It was his way of explaining why so many people keep moving forward when they should stay still. The three rules every lost hiker should know: stay put, stay warm, stay dry. But their heartbeats accelerate, they begin to panic, their emotions take over. She thinks of stories where people drown in three feet of water. They flail wildly, overcome by sheer terror, when all they needed to do was calm down and stand up. Lost hikers are the same. They begin to go even faster, desperate to get there. It's just around the bend; it's just over that ridge. The physical strain takes its toll, dulls their minds. In this way they take themselves from temporary confusion to deeply lost. Only they don't admit it to themselves. For starters, they can't quite believe it, Makayla muses. They don't want to believe it. And it's the denial that brings them deeper into trouble. But eventually, they know. The stark awareness of that single fact—*lost in the wild!*—hits like a sledgehammer.

The ranger pauses. She drinks through a hose connected to her Camelbak. Loves that thing. Small sips all day long. She shifts the backpack on her shoulders, tightens the belt to take more of the weight on her hips. She's back thinking about the weather service information. A minor cold front. Nothing severe, but cold and wet is a recipe for hypothermia. Even in the summer, it can get chilly some nights. Especially if they're underprepared. Staying dry, that's number one. Then they can deal with the cold. If they get wet . . . it's hard to ever feel warm again. A person with early stages of hypothermia gets a case of what rangers call "the umbles." They fumble, stumble, mumble. The brain not working right. They have a hard time walking, talking, doing simple tasks like zipping a coat. After that, the body shuts down. It's over.

She remembers the expression used by survivalists. *You can go three minutes without air, three hours without warmth, three days without water, and three weeks without food.* That's basically about right.

An eleven-year-old boy.

A thirteen-year-old girl.

Out there somewhere.

Still alive, she figures.

It's late summer. If it were colder, they'd already be dead.

So what was she thinking? Oh, yes. That horrible moment when they realize they are lost. As things become more unfamiliar, some hikers in that position totally freak. They run and scramble and do risky things. Others just give up. Those are the ones who are dead within forty-eight hours. She checks her watch. By Makayla's reckoning, it's already been more than fifty hours, but no more than sixty. There's not a real lot of time left. This thought gets her on the move again, taking on altitude now, the trail abruptly more vertical.

"Where are you?" she whispers out loud.

And then: *I hope you're smart.*

She pauses, cups her hands, calls out again.

Listens.

Keeps walking.

[CARTER]

That night, the trees of the forest began talking.

Carter overhears their murmuring.

Of course, he knows little of trees and nothing of their primordial tongue. To his ears it is only wind through the moonlit, shimmering leaves. He doesn't comprehend that roots intermingle, that electrical impulses pass from root tip to root tip, tree to tree, in a vast unfathomable social network of interconnected forest. How all trees of the forest are *one* tree continuous. A community, an underground wood-wide web. Carter hears the moan of a heavy branch, the groan of another, and the sporadic signals of tree parts dropped to the ground: sticks, stems, detritus falling all around him, delivering messages in a complex code. If these sounds were translated into words from a human world, Carter still could not grasp their meaning, as foreign to him as the tongue of a lost tribe. No boy can talk to trees.

Time is different for trees and rocks and the human species. Trees live for decades, centuries; generations pass through in a continuous ecosystem through the ages. Trees have existed on the planet since long before the first hominids walked upright, and trees will remain long after humankind is wiped off the earth's surface. A smudge on a windowpane. The great trees persist, and wait, and watch, and whisper.

Alone and cold and closing in on hypothermia in the wild

unknown, the boy half hears below consciousness the sounds of the trees—those feral, nighttime communications of the wood makers, the carbon eaters, the sunseekers, the water gulpers. From the beginning, roots have turned toward the things they desired: water, nutrient-rich soil, a firmer grip. Beneath Carter, below the understory, the roots of the forest send out messages to one another.

The trees are talking about the boy.

It is time.

Long limbs reach toward him.

33

[LIFT]

In his fever, shivering cold and yet somehow his body a furnace of fire, Carter's scrambled mind recalls stories. The tales from his earliest days, just a small boy in his parents' bed, listening as his mother's voice dances across the ceiling, drifts down the windows like rainwater, seals his eyes shut.

He remembers the story of how Jack's mother sent the boy on a long journey to the marketplace to sell their last cow, to save what was left of the family. No father around, Carter remembers now, so the terrible mission was left to the boy. Was there a dog in that tale?

Carter drifts toward that unknown land. He asks himself if there was a sister in the story. Was she alone and afraid, too? And in his fevered visions, Carter dreams of Grace and Jack, impossibly linked together in the same tall tale.

The story of Jack—foolish Jack!—leaps electrically across synapses. How he traded the last cow for six magic seeds. Swindled, cheated, robbed! His mother, Jack's mother, not *his* mother, furiously scattering the seeds out the window. The family ruined! All lost! A sister forsaken. The mother cries, "We'll never survive now!"

Oh how they cried and cried. How does Carter recall this story? Is it stored somewhere in his mind, one item in a warehouse of dust? Does it float in a cloud of collective unconsciousness?

Does he venture up to retrieve it, even now, in his feverish dream? Or does the story come for him unbidden? Does the tale seek him out and submerge through his skin? Like a message rooted out from some dark understory.

Come, listen.

Let us tell you a tale about a boy named Jack.

And the seeds do grow. Up and up to impossible heights. Climb the beanstalk, Jack. Only do this one impossible thing. Don't look down, don't imagine your failure, the epic fall. Cling tight. Pull with your tired arms, strain with the stretched and weary ligaments of your back, push your trembling legs. Strive with your quivering heart.

Climb higher, higher.

Carter senses the ground fall away from him. Incredible—falling *from*, not *to*—falling up!—the earth dropping away as he is lifted skyward. Carter's eyes roll. It is full dark. With each silent step, the stars above roll like waves. He is staring up into a dark sea swimming with stars. Carter senses a heartbeat, warmth, the cradle of two arms carrying him through a maze of trees. A great, hairy beard.

The angular man does not speak. But he makes a sound, a thrum, as if consoling a baby bird that has fallen from its nest, an orphaned robin—*There, there*, the noise says, *there, there*—and the boy is carried by the man to his home place.

Carter's mind powers down to nothingness, an uncharged phone, dreamless and gray as granite. Head lolling, eyes glimpse the blur of beard, the serious moonlight, his salvation.

Carter moans one word: "Grace."

34

[PREY]

I n the darkest hour, when screeching owls stalk their prey and rip heads off mice, a scent causes Sitka to stir. She stands, tail up, nostrils flared. She noisily snorts out the air, clearing the passageway for the next deep sniff. The animal steps forward. A low rumble comes from her chest, a worried growl. Her body vibrates, trembles. She puts forth a low woof.

Know me, it says to the wilderness.

Grace wakens. "What is it, girl?" Her voice an urgent whisper. She cannot see a hand before her face. She grabs the flashlight. Tries to turn it on. Wait, that's off. Now on. Off, on. She shakes it, the batteries rattle, dead. No light.

The dog's chest is out, the raised hair on her back makes Sitka appear larger, tail straight up, more formidable.

Something out there.

Padding soundlessly in the dark.

"What is it, girl? What do you smell?" Grace struggles to her feet, standing on one leg, propped against the wall.

The dog cannot answer, yet knows she is being *asked* something, hears the amalgam of fear and urgency in the timorous human voice, smells the spike in the girl's cortisol and adrenaline. Sitka knows when things are normal and when they are not.

Sitka is on high alert. She smells the world in telling details, pinpoints, sharp specifics—not a wash of indistinguishable odors.

The dog smells everything, recent past and the acute present, for a mile in all directions, depending on air currents. The data overload is immense. Mind-boggling to process. But one odor comes clearest. Though Sitka has no direct experience of "mountain lion," that named thing, something in her DNA recognizes the lurking danger, the predator prowling in the dark, unseen and unheard.

But not unsmelled.

Therefore: known.

An old enemy.

Sitka vacuums in the odors, sifts through the information. The creatures with names she cannot know: squirrel, vole, owl, mole, mouse, rabbit, hawk, raccoon. Another faint whiff troubles the dog: man. A desperate man has recently moved through this area, the aroma of stealth and haste.

And another thing: the trees themselves, hosts to so much life. Tree limbs and tree fingers, tree thoughts and tree intentions. The interconnected roots, thirsty and entangled, talking in their ancient tongues, passing along what they know to each other. This is the wild place, the space of time-before, and now the dog forgets recent pleasures of soft cushions and screen doors, fresh water bowls and proffered treats, long drives with the windows down.

Dog recalls wolf.

The time-before.

The snaggletooth. The vicious bite and muzzle shake. The primal memory of ripped flesh and the warm taste of red blood. The fresh kill.

"What do you smell?" Grace asks.

How does the dog answer?

Sitka sits alert, rumbles low, hackles raised, muscles taut. *Danger*, her body replies.

She senses danger.

Grace's hands blindly reach into the backpack. She unzips the medical kit. *Where is it? Where is it?* Sitka growls louder, barks low. Grace remembers putting the whistle in the pocket of her flannel, finds it, and blows. She blows and blows, shrill and piercing, and does not stop until she is raw, fractured, spent.

She sags to the ground, exhausted and jangled. She lies on her side, chest wheezing, and stares unblinking into the black.

Sitka finally lowers to the ground, front paws out, head still high, nose working.

Trembling in fear.

This is how the third night passes.

DAY 4

[GRACE]

Dawn's foreshadowing of sunrise. Early light. A soft gray glow at first, like a reverse echo of a sound to come: a lightening of darkness. The broken spine of night. Not light, not the sun's honeyed rays arrowing through the trees, but the foreshadowing of light—a promise whispered in Grace's ear.

Light is coming, and with it, a new day.

Grace watches unmoving as the dark woods gradually take on space, contour, color, dimension. The shapes of tree trunks, movement in the branches, squirrels chittering and birds with their insistent, *I'm here, I'm here, I'm here!*

The trees come alive with birds and their words.

Today springs from yesterday, the dream of tomorrow becomes the new now, and inside Grace's chest an ember still glows. Call it hope. Call it fierce will. Grace is determined to live. Somehow. Someway. She is alone and injured, her infection blackening, one girl in the vastness of a mountain wilderness. Somewhere, she hopes, Carter is okay. He never should have left. A terrible decision. Grace begins to feel that tug of negativity, her thoughts going down a dark path, but she fights against them in the same way a falling figure claws against gravity. She senses that negative thinking will not sustain her here. *Carter will find a way*, she resolves. *My job is to survive.*

Grace closes her eyes and prays. It has never seemed to do

much good in the past. Honestly, she isn't all that sure. But prayer is a meeting of soul and intention. Her prayer does not require answers. Grace has never understood how some people claim to talk with God or how he answered their prayers. This new morning, Grace does not expect a reply. It is enough to think the words, to bring unity of spirit and mind, the meeting of wish and desire— like a corked bottle with a rolled-up note inside, floating in a great, unpeopled sea.

Sending the note is enough.

I am here.

I have survived so far.

I would love with all my heart to see another day.

[SLEEP]

Carter stirs, groans.

He rolls from his back to his side, feels a weight covering his body. He's warm, hot almost. Covered up in blankets or something.

He senses movement nearby. A presence. The night itself, breathing in, breathing out.

"Grace," he moans.

"Sleep," a voice replies.

Carter sleeps.

[THE CAMP]

Carter finds himself sipping warm liquid from a metal coffee cup. His lips feel cracked, but the beverage goes down his throat and fills his belly. He sits comfortably on a rock and the sun falls on his head and shoulders. He's lost his cap.

A bearded man, wearing camouflage pants and a dark green, long-sleeve shirt, stands nearby. His arms are crossed. His lace-up boots look battered and dirty. The man walks away, crouches to the ground, his back to Carter. He's busy with something. A faint metallic sound. Carter closes his eyes, his hands wrapped around the cup, feels the steam rise up into his nostrils. Still dazed, his thoughts can't quite come together.

The man walks over, holds out a tin bowl of chili.

"Eat," he says.

Carter sets down the cup on the dirt floor. He accepts the bowl into his hands. Everything in slow motion. He stares at it, confused. "Do you have . . . a spoon?"

The man makes a sound with his mouth. Turns, walks, bends, returns with a spoon. He does not speak.

Carter looks up at the man, who does not meet his eyes. He seems to be looking somewhere above and to the left of Carter's hunched body. The man has long, thinning hair—flecked with gray—that splays down to his shoulders. *Maybe thirty, forty years old*, Carter figures. It's hard to tell, like telling the age of one of these trees. Carter shudders from a momentary chill, realizes he has a wool shirt draped over his back. He can scarcely speak. "Thanks," he rasps.

Begins spooning the food into his mouth. He does this steadily until the bowl is empty. The man takes it all—the bowl, spoon, and cup—and walks across the small clearing. There's a large, two-galloon, clear plastic container tucked into the bushes. The man silently works, rinses the utensils, places them on a rock to dry.

Carter lifts his head, looks around more closely. They are in a small, tight clearing. It feels like a large cocoon. There are two massive boulders on one side, about a shoulder's width apart. A mass of dense shrubs and trees press inward from every direction. The undergrowth bursts with ferns. Somewhere a woodpecker hammers for grubs. Cicadas whir.

He's a guest in this man's orderly, spartan campsite. But Carter sees no ring of stones, no firepit, no charred wood. Across the way, a crude kitchen: a metal box, a small camping stove, and—so impossible that Carter can't quite believe his eyes—a propane tank, camouflaged with green and brown duct tape. Different items hang from nails in a tree: bungee cords, green plastic bags, wire, a jug filled with water, a dustpan, and a whisk broom.

Carter finds it hard to concentrate, feels light-headed and weak. He absorbs the calm of the environment, the natural hush, the soporific sound of the breeze stirring the leaves. He yawns, utterly spent. It is as if the blood in his body slows as it passes through his veins, like a gawking driver by a roadside wreck.

"Is this where you live?" Carter rouses himself to ask.

The man ignores him.

The site doesn't look right to Carter. There's something off about it.

"Why here?" the boy asks.

The man turns, looks in his inquisitor's direction. "Privacy," he says. Terse and sharp.

An inner alarm clangs deep in Carter's core. He sits perfectly still, feeling its reverberation on the hairs of his neck. He realizes they are perfectly closeted away in this place. *Hidden.*

Behind him, Carter spies a dark, horizontal crevice in the ground. Like a hollowed-out tomb. There's a deep-green tarp above it, a disorderly jumble of branches. He knows this is where he slept. The man now holds out a damp cloth. Water drips from his long fingers. "For your face," he says.

Carter's left eye is nearly swollen shut. It doesn't hurt; it doesn't matter, it just adds to his fog. He lifts his face to the man who, in reply, steadies Carter with a firm grip on the top of his skull. It's like he's palming a basketball. With the other hand, he presses the cloth on Carter's insect-ravaged forehead, cheeks, lips, jawline, neck.

"You'll get used to it," the man says.

His hands are huge.

Carter yawns, feels the warm food in his stomach, yawns again. He can't seem to stay awake.

"My sister," he begins.

"Not now," the man replies. He gestures to the hole in the ground. "Rest."

Carter doesn't argue.

He can barely stand.

He crawls back into the narrow hole, the shape of a lozenge, which is surprisingly warm and comfortable. He is asleep in seconds.

38

[TRY]

U sing the walking stick as a crutch, Grace hops and painfully hobbles to the water source. She fills the bottle, rinses her face, arms, legs. It pleases her to obtain water in this way. Not just absently turning a faucet, opening the fridge. Despite her injuries, the act connects Grace to this place. An intricate spiderweb, damp with dew, sparkles in the ferns. The slightest effort exhausts her, so she takes it slow. There's no need to rush. Oh, yes, a hot shower would be so sweet right now. Body wash, sweet-smelling shampoo, just an hour with her phone. Her mind feels clear this morning. The sky, too, is a crisp, polished blue. A few puffy clouds that look deliciously edible. She admires the orange-yellow wildflowers. There are rows of conical purple ones, too. Life abounds. Grace sees shiny black berries on a bush about her height. The leaves are oval in shape, pointed at one end. She wonders if she could eat them. Or are they poisonous? Food is definitely an issue. She thinks of survival shows where naked people in the woods eat bugs. She'd do it, she decides, if it comes to that. It would be disgusting—but Grace realizes she needs protein. Just not today.

How many days is it? She's not sure. Counts and whispers aloud, *"Four."*

She squats and pees right there. No point being modest. Her mind travels back the years to a memory from when she was a little girl. Four years old? Five years old? It's difficult to say. Her father was laid up, recovering from a serious motorcycle accident. Out riding his beloved Harley—he enjoyed "tooling around" on weekends—he hit some gravel on a hairpin turn. The back wheel lost traction, skidded, and the bike fell, crushing his right leg.

He was determined to recover without a limp. So the doctor devised a plan. He explained to Grace's father that many people limp because they favor the leg. It hurts, so they are reluctant to put their full weight on the injured limb. Thus, they never regain full strength, form a habit, and walk with a limp.

The doctor told Mr. Taylor, "If you follow my instructions each day without fail, you will recover fully. No limp. It's up to you."

It became a game. He handed Grace a digital stopwatch. He would take his position in the hallway, steady himself against the wall. Then he would nod to Grace, lift his left leg off the ground, and stand with his full weight on the injured leg. At the beginning, he could stand it for five seconds, ten seconds. A little more each day. She'd watch as he stood, sweat forming above his lip, face gone flushed, his body trembling with determination. "How long?" he'd ask, still holding the pose.

Grace learned to call out the intervals. "Forty-five seconds . . . sixty seconds . . . seventy-five . . ."

He would stand until he could stand no longer, and then he would stand a bit longer than that. Toward the end of each session, Mr. Taylor looked depleted, haggard. He'd nod, not even smiling, take a deep breath, and say, "Again."

This period signaled the end of his daredevil days, no more

rides on the Harley, and the beginning of his prodigious belly. But he never did limp.

Grace resolves to stand. The tenderness of her ribs becomes a sharp, sudden, stabbing pain when she makes certain movements. She gets to her knees, blows the air out, breathes in. Reaches to the ground with her left hand for balance, tucks in her toes, counts—*three, two, one*—and in one excruciating motion comes to her feet. An involuntary cry comes from her mouth. Sitka paces nearby, agitated. The dog comes to Grace, presses a moist nose against the back of her knee, whines softly. Grace blinks away the pain. Her right foot, the sprained or shattered ankle, softly kisses the ground. A whisper. Almost all of Grace's weight is placed on her left foot. She stands shakily, her hand on the firmly planted walking stick.

"Okay," she says out loud.

Sitka listens.

"That was fun," she says. "Now for the hard part."

Grace gradually transfers more and more weight to her right leg. The pain is immense and seems to shoot through her entire body. She feels dizzy, light-headed. And yet she persists until she is standing solidly on two feet. The stick is lifted in the air.

She remembers her father in the hallway. Stares off to the middle distance, focuses on a sturdy oak, and now lifts her left foot off the ground. She stands entirely on the damaged leg. Grace counts, "Five . . . four," and surrenders. She bends, gasping for air, one hand on a knee, the other leaning on the stick. The pain in her chest returns, a knife twisting about six inches below her right armpit.

Grace nods, lightly touches the dog's head, runs her fingers the length of Sitka's ears. She rises up to full height, focuses once more on the mighty oak, and says:

"Again."

Again, and again.

[JOHN]

Carter blinks, remembers.

I've been saved.

But he is not sure by whom, exactly.

Feigning sleep, Carter secretly looks out from the coffinlike comfort of his sleeping quarters, watches the wiry man sitting on the rock in absolute stillness. His shirtless back is to Carter, his head turned to the right in a downward-seeming gaze. He wears sleeves of tattoos on both arms and ink on his back. Perhaps he is lost in thought, staring intensely at nothing whatsoever. Ghosts, maybe? Carter sees the lines around the man's eyes. His sun- and rain- and wind-weathered face. The man's great beard displays a montage of colors: brown with patches of red, streaks of gray.

"You're awake," the man says, without turning his head.

Somehow he knew.

Carter climbs out, stands, stretches like a cat. "How long did I sleep?"

The man shrugs. Points to the sky. "There's the clock."

Carter glances up, confused, then gets it. Oh, the sun. At least he knows it's daytime. "What were you doing?" Carter asks.

"Doing?"

"Sitting there," Carter says.

The man scowls through his beard. He rises, gestures to the rock for Carter to sit. He goes to the kitchen area, digs around, returns with an old plastic bowl filled with brown rice. Hands it to Carter. He mutters something, shakes his head. Goes back and gets a fork.

Carter thanks him and shovels forkfuls of cold rice into his mouth. He's never eaten plain rice before and now wonders why not. It is delicious. The perfect meal.

"Do you even want to know my name?" Carter asks.

"Names," the man echoes. He swats away a fly.

"It's Carter. Carter Aaron Taylor. My sister is Grace. She's still out there and we have to—"

"We don't 'have to' anything," the man spits back. He rises, tugs a long-sleeve shirt over his lean, undernourished torso. He paces in an agitated state of distress, across and back. Five long strides. Sparks almost leap off his body, like struck steel just out of the furnace.

Carter waits for the storm to pass.

Finally, the angular man stops, looks in the direction of Carter but doesn't quite meet his eyes. He takes a deep breath. Gives a "settle down" motion with his hands. "Just—don't—push," he warns.

It frightens Carter, the way the man says it. There's an undercurrent of anger. This isn't normal. Grace is still out there. She needs help. He'll have to be more careful. There's something wild jumping around in this guy's eyes.

"John," the man finally confides. He smiles to himself, as if remembering a joke. He's trying, in his way, to defuse the charged atmosphere. "How old?"

"Eleven," Carter answers. "And . . . thanks."

The man appears genuinely baffled. Shakes his head. He admits, "I'm not a big raconteur."

The look on Carter's face is blank.

"I don't talk much," he explains.

Carter doesn't say: *Well, dude, you're alone.* Instead, he finishes the bowl, walks it over toward the kitchen area.

"Don't," the man says. "Give it here."

Carter hands over the fork and bowl. "Sorry, I was just trying—"

"Don't means *don't*," John snaps. "I don't need a story to go with it. Don't you understand how dangerous this is? Keep your head down, kid. They're watching our every move." He tosses the bowl to ground, kicks it. The bowl bounces off the boulder and into the twisted arms of a scarlet-berried bush.

Carter stands still, helplessly watching. He doesn't know what else to do.

"I didn't anticipate this," the man says. A vein in his forehead visibly pulses. "This is not—I never thought—you'd make it out of the bog."

Carter sags to his seat on the rock. *The bog.* His brain's not fully back. As if a piece of his spirit is still stuck in that low place. A sliver of self left out there, sinking in the muck. The man's words register. "You saw me?"

"I carried you here, didn't I?"

"Yes, but . . . ," Carter says. He rubs his forehead. "I don't remember anything. I mean, when I was in the bog. Were you watching me?"

The man frowns through his beard. His eyes dart. "Just be glad you're alive."

Carter tells him the story. How they came here. His father, his sister. How they planned to hike Blood Mountain. Every detail. He might as well be talking to a tree. John says little.

Minutes pass. Carter remembers the tattoos on John's back and arms. Eagles and skulls and a tattered flag. Words and hearts and barbed wire. "You were a soldier?" he asks.

John looks at him, says nothing, but his eyes provide the answer.

"Where?" Carter asks.

"Doesn't matter," John replies.

"Okay," Carter says. "I'm just making conversation."

John shakes his head. "You talk a lot."

Carter smiles, undeterred. "My mom says I should be a lawyer, on account of I talk so much."

John doesn't feel compelled to keep the conversation going. He looks up into the trees, as if forgetting Carter is even there. He's a man alone again. Not waiting, not thinking. Just . . . being. Like another plant that has taken root and risen up from the ground.

"That must have been a long time ago, right?" Carter says. The man isn't a kid. Carter is still guessing midthirties. Hard to tell. He gives no answer.

Carter prods, "Wasn't it?"

"Not to me, it wasn't," John says. "Feels like yesterday."

The sharp cheekbones of his face above the beard, the haunted look of his eyes, tells Carter that it's true. For this former soldier, the war continues. He brought it back home.

A plane flies high overhead. Both watch it draw a white line across the blue sky.

"I need to get help for my sister," Carter says. "Can you help me, John? Please?"

After a long silence, John answers, "That's not possible."

"*You're* not possible," Carter weakly answers back. "My sister is hurt. She has no food. She might be—" Carter stops, shakes his head. He shifts in his seat, and changes his strategy. "I can't do it without your help."

"I saved you once," John says.

"So," Carter says.

"Don't make me regret it. Be glad you're alive."

"Yeah, like you, right?" Carter says.

John looks away. Picks up a leaf. Quietly shreds it in his hands. He stands and walks away.

"Where you going?" Carter asks. "John?"

The angular man stops, points a finger. "You. Stay."

"John?"

The man glares, angry at the world.

"What? I'm trapped here?" Carter asks.

"Tomorrow," he answers. "Today, you rest." He slips off through the narrow gap between the two rock boulders.

[SEARCH]

Makayla sings as she hikes. Usually it's Marvin Gaye, Al Green, Mavis Staples, the old soul classics that her parents played in their apartment. Flatbush Avenue, Brooklyn, New York, a world away. Singing is both habit and comfort. In bear country, it's advised to make noise on the trail. Some hikers even carry bells to avoid surprising any mama bears with their cubs. The wild things don't want to mess with humans. Makayla thinks of the escaped mountain lion. This cat might be ruined. No sign of it yet. Very unlikely it's out and about in the late afternoon. At the same time, it's no ordinary lion. Spent its life in a cage. What does it know?

Ever since Makayla learned the name of the missing girl, the tune wormed into her skull and would not crawl out. She used to sing it loud and proud as a child at Sunday service, dressed in frilly whites, clutching her mama's hand:

> *Amazing grace, how sweet the sound,*
> *I hear You singing over me,*
> *I once was lost, but now I'm found . . .*

The ranger stops to take in the contours of the landscape. Scans for irregularities. A color or shape that doesn't belong. She tries to imagine the bad decision a lost child might make. On instinct, she veers off to follow a deer trail. Checks her cell phone: dead zone. No surprise there. She pulls out the map, calls into dispatch on the hand radio, relays her coordinates. Over and out.

She picks up the song like a loose thread, never missing a beat:

> *My soul is silent, I am found,*
> *And it's a beautiful sound.*
> *It's a beautiful, beautiful sound.*

For the Department of Environmental Conservation, today is considered day two of the operational period. It was set in motion yesterday, the moment Makayla called in the discoveries she made at the trailhead. Strong suspicion of two children lost. But for her, the search began in earnest when her boots first hit the trail. Those kids had a two-day head start.

The search-and-rescue operation was extensive, organized, and highly motivated—now bumped up to incorporate type 3 strategies. Working in coordination with the state police, the DEC planned to throw every available resource at it. Lieutenant Watkins drove in from the suboffice and was personally directing the show at the mobile command post. Multiple rangers were actively involved and, last Makayla heard, they'd already received responses from more than eighty volunteers. More would follow. These weren't just ordinary citizens wandering around with flashlights, calling "Yoo-hoo"; the department held regular training sessions to certify volunteers in search methods and procedures. These were smart outdoorspeople, experienced men and women, wise to the ways of the backcountry. They did invaluable work. Still, organizing that many was no simple task. Working a search grid, a type 3 technique, took strict efficiency and constant oversight. Makayla was glad it wasn't her assignment; she far preferred running trails out in the field. Even with all those resources at play, sometimes hikers don't get found right away. Days can turn into weeks. Optimism morphs into something darker. Today's afternoon cloud cover wasn't helping. Days started out clear, but not anymore. Due to poor visibility, aviation was grounded because the weather was deemed "not conducive."

Makayla was freelancing. Working independently, trusting instincts sharpened on the whetstone of personal experience. She's not scheduled to take a shift the next two days, actually has longstanding plans to visit her boyfriend, so Makayla pushes extra hard today. She stops, calls, whistles, glasses the landscape for any signs. The dog might be her best hope. And of the three, the one most imperiled. Good thing the dog was a mutt. Most purebreeds would never make it out here. She whistles again. An image comes to her, that long silver, slender whistle in the glove compartment, and she tucks away the idea for later. Maybe Frank can help with that. Makayla notices a shrub growing from fleshy roots just five feet away. It has attractive, glossy, black berries. She recognizes the shrub as *Atropa belladonna*, deadly nightshade. An invasive species native to Europe, Northern Africa, and Asia. Somehow it got into Canada and now here. Such is life in the shrinking world. She read the other day how disease-carrying bacteria attach itself to floating plastic and cross oceans—it survives for years, suckered to a tossed soda bottle—changing the course of continents in the process. The invasive berries might look appetizing, but they are poisonous. She hopes Grace and Carter have enough sense not to eat anything they aren't sure about.

Dispatch relays a message. Turns out the heart attack victim, Mr. Taylor, has been upgraded from critical to stable condition. "Looks like he's going to make it," the voice on the radio informs her. He's asking about his kids. This cheers Makayla. It gives fresh bounce to her step. Good news always does.

[ROCK THOUGHTS]

There is so much Grace doesn't know about rocks and plants and birds and mountains. It is as if she is a visitor to a foreign land who doesn't speak the language. She knows *tree* but not butternut from elm, oak from alder, beech from ash. They are mysterious words drifting in her mind, like jellyfish in a great sea, attached to nothing, and therefore meaningless. Lost words disconnected from the world. It has never mattered to her before: the names of things. But in this place, her home-for-now, surrounded by these living creatures—breathing, swaying, sighing— Grace senses she has missed something essential. She is filled with regret. Grace says to Sitka, "When we get back, I'm going to learn all about this place. The names of everything." The dog, lying on her side in the shade, drums her tail on the ground. Sitka lifts her head, not to look at the girl but to turn her nose in the speaker's direction. Her ears lift, too.

"And I also want to say," Grace tells the dog, "thank you for staying with me. You are the best good girl in the world, yes, you are." An expression pops into Grace's mind: *I'd be lost without you*. It almost makes her laugh, thinking: *Oh well, I guess I'm lost with you!*

Sitka languidly rises, the early stages of arthritis in her joints. She is weakened by the heat of the day, and from a lack of nutrition, and by her responsibilities in this new world. The near-constant vigilance. Tail relaxed, the dog moves closer to Grace. The girl is sitting up in her now-familiar position, her back propped against the rock wall. Grace pats the ground, here. The dog collapses wearily in that very spot, her curled back pressing against Grace's thigh. Grace rests her hand on the animal, and like that they affirm their connection: you and me, together in this place. A sharp pain reminds Grace of her battered ribs when she shifts her legs or adjusts the position of her back. Actually, it only hurts when she breathes. Oh well. Grace closes her eyes, counts slowly—*one, two, three, four, five*—and waits for the wave of pain to subside. There, better. She is learning to manage it.

How, even, do mountains happen? She does not know. Grace knows only that there is rock, strangely, exactly here. How or why it got here she doesn't comprehend. Grace reaches up with her left arm, the one that is less sore, and feels the coolness of the flat rock against the back of her hand. Again, mystically: flooded with gratefulness and communion.

Inspired, Grace limp-hops down a few feet to more closely examine nature. She tries to think like a naturalist. This plant has small round leaves bunched in threes. This rock is jagged, not smooth. That tree's wrinkled bark reminds her of an elephant's knees. She decides to make up her own names for things.

"This plant," she tells her four-legged companion, "is called heartwort. It heals broken hearts, makes sadness disappear. But one must stare at it for a long, long time for its magical properties to take effect."

The dog sits sphinxlike on its belly, front left paw stretched out, attentive.

"And that tree," Grace continues. "Now what is that one called?"

At the rise of her voice, the inflection at the end of the sentence, the dog tilts her head as if puzzling out the answer.

"Do you give up, girl?" Grace asks. "That's called a starscraper. Don't you see that long straight trunk, the way the uppermost branches reach toward the sky? Oh yes, that's a starscraper all right. The stars like to have their bellies scratched, just like you." Grace reaches over to scratch the dog around the head and neck. Sitka's fur is thick and matted. Grace picks at it, grooming the dog.

Grace gestures to the collection of medium-size stones that she has painstakingly gathered into a small pile. Her arsenal in case of attack. "These are called getouttaheres," Grace explains. "They are perfect for throwing at wild beasties." She holds one in her palm, weighs the heft of it, turns it around in her fingers. "They are also called stone wasps. They sting."

Grace looks away, lost in the thought. She wonders if a handful of stones could possibly protect her from an attack. Probably not, she decides. By that point it might be too late. Perhaps a good strike on the snout might be enough to give the attacker some pause, time enough to wonder if it's worthwhile to engage with a creature that stings from a distance. She worries most about bears.

"Maybe that's all I need," Grace tells Sitka, "just enough to warn them not to mess with me."

[SHREDS]

C arter is unsure of what to do. At first, he idly waits, expecting the man who saved his life to return. The minutes drag. Carter tries to figure out how to use the sun to estimate the hour of day. He holds his right hand straight up. Twelve o'clock. High noon. But the sun isn't up there. It seems to be inclining toward the horizon. Long past noon. He extends his left arm to the side, parallel to the ground. That's the horizon. Sunset, right? Call that eight o'clock. Looking up, he sees the sun is almost perfectly at the midpoint between the directions indicated by his two hands. *Four o'clock*, he thinks, *best guess*.

It settles the essential question: To stay or go? The memory of yesterday feels like a sandbag in his chest. He can't face that again. Can't risk it. Especially not this late in the afternoon. He is afraid of becoming lost again.

Carter tries to convince himself that he needs to rest, recover his strength. He's not ready to make that kind of hike. Not after what just happened in the bog. *Tomorrow*, John had said. But Carter doesn't trust him. Something about John feels deeply, disturbingly wrong.

Carter slips through the narrow space between the two boulders. It's tight even for Carter. He has to sidestep his way through. He takes about five steps beyond the rock. That's all the open space available. When he turns, the effect is astonishing. Due to the position of the rocks, one slightly in front of the other, there's no visible crack. The two boulders would appear to anyone walking by as one impassible rock wall. And what hiker would walk by? There's no path. Carter can't imagine which way John might have gone.

Something alerts his senses. Carter strains to listen. The birds have quieted. Even the ever-present white noise of cicadas seems strangely absent. He feels uneasy, as if he's being observed.

No, not watched. Stalked.

He glances around. The terrain is so thick with chaotic growth, he can't see more than ten feet in any direction.

"Hello?" he asks.

Waits.

"John?"

The wilderness does not reply.

If he ventures any farther, Carter isn't sure he'd find his way back again. Not without cairns or trail markers. Hansel and Gretel used bread crumbs, but they got lost because birds ate them. Still, it gives Carter the beginning of an idea. A way to probe the wilderness but safely find his way back if necessary. He retreats back through the crack.

Nothing to do but wait.

He investigates the camp more fully. He drinks from the water bag that hangs by a strap from the tree. Hungry, he finds a metal locker tucked into the brush, next to the propane tank. Inside there's a number of neatly stacked plastic containers and glass jars: rice, oats, grain, nuts, dried fruit. He opens a jar of almonds. Chomps on a few. There's a jar of peanut butter. He wishes for bread. And in another jar—*can it be?*—candy corn. Yellow and orange triangles of pure sugar. Not at all what he expected. Carter twists the lid, steals a few. They taste like Halloween, like home. He carefully returns everything to its well-ordered place.

Under a tarp he finds a canvas bag stuffed with John's crisply folded clothes. A heavy shirt, socks, etcetera. There's something else: a well-worn, wrinkled copy of a book. Poems by Lao Tzu. The pages are dog-eared, with lines underlined. Opens to a random page and reads:

> *The five colors*
> *Blind our eyes.*
> *The five notes*
> *Deafen our ears.*

Whatever. Carter flips to a new page:

> *Who knows*
> *Doesn't talk.*
> *Who talks*
> *Doesn't know.*

Carter doesn't understand it, but realizes the words must be important to John. He turns to the first poem, "Taoing."

> *The way you can go*
> *Isn't the real way.*
> *The name you can say*
> *Isn't the real name.*
> *Heaven and earth*
> *Begin in the unnamed.*

Whoa. He tucks the book back into the bag. He fingers his way through the clothes. Toward the bottom, he spies a red cloth, pulls it out. It's a bandanna. Perfect.

While hunting around beyond the perimeter for a safe spot to hide the borrowed bandanna, Carter stumbles upon a hole in the ground. He very nearly falls in it. Branches had covered it. When he removes them, it reveals a small square pit framed with logs. Carter peers in, sniffs, rears back. *It must be where he goes,* Carter realizes. Sealed nearby in a plastic garbage bag, a large plastic spoon and a white chemical powder that smells like fertilizer. He lays the branches back in place, as if undisturbed. He already knows this about John. Everything in its place.

Carter returns to the sitting rock, the thinking rock, and tries to solve the puzzle of this man. The camp is spare, yet it doesn't feel temporary to Carter. One look at the sleeping quarters—painstakingly prepared, warm and dry and astonishingly comfortable—suggests to Carter that John has slept here many, many nights.

Weeks. Months.

A current of unease ripples through him.

He decides to eat more candy corn.

He notices again the utensils. One cup, one bowl. Scrub pad. A spoon, fork, knife.

Carter tests the knife's sharpness against the palm of his hand. Nice and sharp. He pockets it and retrieves the bandanna. He brings the items into his sleeping area, safely out of sight should John suddenly arrive, and begins to shred.

43

[VULTURES]

John feels jittery, distracted. He walks, muttering to himself, mind racing. He didn't want the boy. But what was he supposed to do? Let him die? And now the kid was already jangling his nerves. Had to get out of there. John figures he might as well resupply. He's got three caches well concealed in different zones. The particular one he wants in Zone D requires extra precaution. Usually, he wouldn't attempt it in daylight. Why risk being seen? His primary goal in life is to stay invisible.

He proceeds cautiously, staying off any trails. Search teams will be up and down these mountains. That's a lot of ground to cover. John is glad he thought to gather intelligence from the boy. He said they parked at the Blood Mountain trailhead. The kids went ahead. John reckons that something must have happened to the father. He fell, got sick—something to remove him from the equation. He assumes the trailhead will become the focal point of the search. They'll begin with the main trail, run the spurs, and radiate out from there. Probably establish a grid system. Standard stuff. They like their straight lines and little boxes. John pictures the map with absolute clarity in his mind. He knows every bend and stone and root of it.

The good news is those kids started out in good shape—they covered an impressive distance. John doesn't expect either one to be found. Okay, the girl, maybe. He sets the odds at forty-sixty.

Nobody is finding the boy. That's not an option. His site is well concealed. Almost impossible for anyone to find. The boy complicates life, puts John at risk. He wonders if it was a mistake to leave Carter alone at the camp. Agitated and restless, John made an impulsive move—he had to get out of there. Even so, he calculated that Carter was too scared to go traipsing off one day after nearly dying in the bog. Kid was impressive out there, John had to admit it. Tomorrow will be another story. More forceful measures might be required. Strong rope, perhaps. Some kind of protective cage? John needs to keep the boy from harm's way. He failed before. Not this time.

To the southwest, John sees birds circling at about two hundred feet. Too big to be hawks. He won't use his binoculars in the open, afraid the glass might reflect the sun and give away his position. John counts seven of them. Turkey vultures, he concludes. Big, bald scavengers. Most raptors fly with their wings straight across. Not these guys. Their wings form a V shape. The vultures are not as graceful in the sky as hawks: their wings tend to wobble in the wind. Their feathers are dark brown-black, but the wing tips are lighter, appear silvery from the ground. The giveaway is the head: it is unusually small and red. No feathers from the neck up. John admires the efficiency of that design. If you are going to eat by shoving your head inside a dead carcass, it's probably best not to have feathers mixed up with all the blood and guts.

John studies them and becomes curious. Sees one drop down, then another, followed by the rest. *Found something.* John smiles to himself. He decides to take a look-see. He remembers, most assuredly, the cat print he discovered yesterday. Only one way to know for sure.

He comes upon them gorging themselves on the half-eaten remains of a dead fawn. John shoos them away, waving his arms. Turkey vultures are cowards at heart. Large birds, but not eager for a fight. John stands, arms folded, assessing the scene. It fascinates him, engages his total attention.

The bony-limbed fawn never had a chance. It was probably nibbling on the tasty bud of a wildflower, and then: good night. John moves in a slow, cautious circle. Something very strong, very powerful bit it behind the neck. Serious damage. Deep claw marks along the flanks. He examines the terrain, can see the path where the cat dragged the body. Such strength. That's what they do. Kill and drag and half bury. There's a hole in the fawn, as if it's been carved out like a pumpkin. Gruesome and haunting. The killer had plucked out the animal's heart and other organs. John can see how the cat attempted to conceal its kill, half covered by leaves and ground matter, before the vultures arrived.

He knows the cat will be back to feed again.

Maybe soon.

Can't be far away.

John wishes he had his bow. He could set up right here, upwind, and wait. But: things to do. Thinking of the girl, and of the troublesome dog, he gets an idea. There's still meat on the deer's forelegs. It would make a nice calling card. He grabs one with both hands, pulls and twists, but it's slippery; he takes a breath, plants a foot against the animal's ribs, gets a firmer grip and, *crunch*, the leg snaps off at the knee.

He never hears the ranger coming from the opposite approach until it's almost too late. He spies the dark-green uniform moving behind a copse of small trees. The ranger's purposeful stride. Her wide-brimmed hat. She stops, crouches. Her hand instinctively goes to her gun.

"Grace?" she calls.

He plunges into the underbrush, scoots on hands and knees, darts behind the cover of aspens and beech. He glances back, *sees her see him*, and runs.

She calls but doesn't chase.

He's already gone—still holding the bloody foreleg in his right hand.

44

[STRANGER]

Makayla drags through the end of a frustrating day. She hates failure. She's following another deer trail. Nothing's worked so far. Hasn't seen a single sign. The previous day's rain didn't help. She ruminates on her long-anticipated getaway the next two days. Hard to leave now. Her boyfriend, Kifeda, won't be happy if she cancels on him again. She sighs, picturing his upset face. He's going to have to get used to it.

A new theory is beginning to form in her mind. Everything she's done today has been wrong. Maybe the kids, Grace and Carter, went all the way up to the summit. Maybe they blasted past the turn and never suspected for miles. If so, they might have followed a creek run down the far side of Blood Mountain. All turned inside out. If they just kept going, desperately and mistakenly pushing and pushing, it could have taken them beyond the search grid. Perhaps tomorrow if she works it from an entirely different approach, drives out to an access road close to Long Lake—

She hears a sound up ahead. Very near. A scuffling. The snap of a stick breaking.

Makayla stops, crouches.

"Grace?" she calls.

She unsnaps the holster on her side.

She hears scurrying, like an elk crashing through timber,

glimpses a shape. Makayla rushes to the spot of the deer carcass. Her eyes are on the trees beyond the underbrush. And she sees him: the wild man of the mountain. The man beast, the thief, the recluse. And she knows, straightaway, all the rumors are true.

[TWILIGHT]

A heavy despondency falls upon Grace as nightfall darkens the forest. She had done so well, kept herself busy all day, thinking only positive thoughts. But now sadness descends, covers her like a heavy blanket. Carter left yesterday morning, almost two full days ago. Her little brother. He should have sent help by now. Rescuers should have found . . .

Unless.

Her mind snags on the one word. *Unless, unless, unless.*

He left with practically nothing. A water bottle, one energy bar. A shirt, maybe. Did he imagine he could march out of here as easy as that?

Grace blames herself for allowing him to leave. She didn't argue hard enough. She runs her hands through her oily hair. She becomes aware of the smell of her body, her fetid clothes.

Tears pool in her eyes, stream down her cheeks, lips, and chin. She lets them come. She tastes salt on her tongue. Tells herself, *I'll give myself five minutes. I'll cry my heart out. But just for five minutes.*

There's a persistent weight, deep in her chest. It hurts to breathe. This implacable fear.

How lost becomes loss.

Images of Carter by himself . . .

She breaks it off.

He's eleven years old. Starts middle school in a week. Brave and sweet but . . .

No, she won't think that way.

Can't think that way.

She dries her eyes, surveys her surroundings. The wilderness does not care. Grace slumps over to the hard ground.

"*Oh, Cart,*" she says.

My heart.

She wonders if anyone will find her. And yet knows she's not able to hike out—even if she knew the way. Which she so doesn't. Graces feels waves of pain echo up her legs, into her chest. She feels helpless, hollow, emptied of hope. What would it be like to die here? Could she just curl up, close her eyes? Only trees and rocks to witness her demise.

"Help me," she moans.

She calls for the dog.

Sitka comes instantly, presses close, pushes against the girl's hip. Grace adjusts her body, throws an arm around the warm, sweet dog. "You're my best good dog," she whispers into the fine, soft hairs of the dog's ears. Her words as fragile as soap bubbles. Grace knows these despairing thoughts are the greatest danger she faces. To survive, she must fight them off. *Tomorrow, I'll do better*, she thinks, and drifts into a delicate sleep, jostled like a small craft across troubled waters.

46

[TRUST]

Sitka trawls through the glorious, odor-filled underbrush. More comfortable with each day, the animal moves deeper into the forest. Grace out of sight, sleeping quietly.

Sitka stops, paw frozen in midstep, when a shape steps out from behind the trunk of a large tree, fifty yards away. The figure is still a safe distance away, upwind. Sitka swallows the rumble of a growl in her throat. It is a man. He walks normally, casually, in a friendly manner. His face smiles. Sitka watches, reading the signs. All her life she has honed one skill above all else: how to read humans. What do they want? Where are they going? Who desires to play? Who feels upset? Who might pose a threat?

"Hey, there, dog," the man's voice chimes, his voice soft and melodic. "How are you doing today? Oh, that's good, that's nice. You are a good dog, aren't you?"

The music of his voice is lilting, even in the darkness, and flows gently to Sitka's ears. She watches the stranger draw closer. Sitka looks to the side, uncertain. Grace is far enough away. The dog positions herself firmly between the stranger, this curious, singsong human, and Grace in her den. But the man does not seem to be a threat.

And there is a smell of meat.

"You are a fine-looking dog," the stranger says. He pours forth a burbling stream of words. "How you holding up out here? I bet you're hungry, aren't you? Would you like a treat? Huh, huh? Well, I have something for you. It's sure looks tasty to me. Would you like a treat? Huh, huh?"

This is a phrase Sitka knows by heart. The intonation, the mellifluous patterns and rhythms of the beneficent human tongue. She smells it fully now, blown to her in a gust. Sitka's ears relax, her mouth opens, her lips hang loose. She watches the man as he slowly bends, whispering all along. He places a fawn-colored bone on the ground. Shreds of meat cling to it. There are streaks where white bone shows through. Sitka leans forward, breathes in the aroma. She pants, tongue out, tasting the delicious breeze.

The man stands and watches.

Sitka sits, waits.

When the man retreats a step, Sitka crawls forward. It becomes a dance. A tango of wariness and trust. At last, the man does not need to move farther away. Sitka hurries to snatch up the bone, hips low, eyes never leaving the stranger's face. She carries it away in her mouth, settles after going a safe distance, and chomps hungrily. A gleam of wolf in her eye.

The soldier smiles, content.

Zero dark. Mission accomplished.

He's built trust.

And so disappears back into the forest.

[DREAM]

I t is deep dark when John returns to camp. He moves soundlessly, almost invisibly in the opaque night. Carter lays with eyes open. He closes them. Opens his eyes again. The scene is unchanged. Rolling on his side slightly, a scattering of stars scarcely visible through the gauze of overhead branches. The night overcast with cloud. The stars seemed to have drifted farther away, wandering elsewhere, leaving him behind. Abandoned by the night sky.

John moving around in the dark. Trying to figure out where to sleep. Carter realizes he occupies the man's bed. The air is fresh in his nose and lungs. Somewhere an animal screeches, another screams; one dies so that another may live.

Tomorrow, he thinks.

Tomorrow will be the day.

He's forgotten to return the knife. It is hidden away, covered by his bed of surprisingly soft, long pine needles.

He clings to shreds of cloth, fisted into a ball: his bread crumbs to scatter when he strikes out alone. If he gets lost again, Carter knows he'll need these markers to find his way back. He thinks of them as an astronaut's tether as he explores deep space. Without the shreds marking the trail, he could become disconnected from John's camp. He'd be lost and alone again. The thought terrifies him—even more than staying with John.

Hours later, John bolts awake, stifles a cry. He is back in

the war. He is watching the black-haired boy's life drain out of his body. The child's small, thin, ravaged corpse. Face twisted in anguish. The end, no matter what the circumstances, always comes as a shock. Severed vein and missing limb. There is no stopping the blood. It is everywhere. On the road, on the boy, and in this dream, on John's own hands.

And it feels to John precisely like the thin ice that forms across a shallow winter puddle. A small boy comes to it, taps the ice ever so gently. *Pop*, it cracks. Steps with full weight and the rubber boot goes all the way through. The ice fractures and snaps into a spiderweb of jagged lines.

That's exactly what it feels like to John.

Inside his chest.

All the time.

His shattered heart.

"You okay?" Carter asks, awakened by John's distress.

The wild man of the woods scrambles to all fours, muscles taut; dives to his belly, eyes blazing. There's a large knife in his hand, a shimmer of it in the pale moonlight, sharp tip pointed at Carter. John looks around desperately, assesses the perimeter. He reaches for the penlight below his neck. The thin white beam targets Carter's face. The boy's eyes squint closed.

Carter raises a hand to shield his face. "Hey," he protests. "It's me."

The man stares for another long minute. Uncomprehending. He is here and not here, awake and yet still dreaming. Still in the land of desert sun and sudden, unspeakable horror.

He shuts off the penlight.

"Go to sleep," he hisses.

DAY 5

48

[DOUGHNUTS]

Makayla arrives at the command post shortly after six in the morning, carrying a big box of doughnuts. Frank is seated in a lawn chair outside the van. His uniform looks rumpled. There are dark circles under his eyes. Hasn't been getting much sleep. There's a long folding table on metal legs at his side— and a large coffee mug in his hand.

"Brooklyn! What have you got there?" he greets her.

She raises the box, "I come bearing gifts!"

"Very thoughtful, thank you," he says. "I hope you got some jellies in there. Those are my absolute favorite."

"It's an assortment, Frank."

He stifles a yawn, tilts his head at an empty chair. "Come, sit a minute."

Makayla fixes a cup of coffee, sits. She informs him of her plans for the day.

He leans over the table to look at the map without rising from his seat. Tugs on his ear. Pounds down a jelly doughnut. Wipes his mouth, rather daintily, with the back of his sleeve. "It's a theory," he concludes. "Long shot."

"You don't agree?" Makayla asks.

"No, I think it's possible. But generally, I like to start with the most obvious places and go from there."

Makayla nods. Makes sense.

"I'll talk to the pilots, clue them into your thinking. I could arrange a flyby, if you'd like," he offers. "Weather looks good for this morning at least. Another foggy night, I'm afraid."

"A flyby would be great, sir," Makayla says.

Frank pauses. "Any more thoughts about our bearded friend up there?"

"The mountain man?" Makayla replies. "I'm not sure what to think. He's real, we know that."

Frank looks her in the eye. "Just so you know, all cards on table. The police chief in town, Bannon, he's got a long list of unsolved robberies. Petty stuff. But folks don't like it, makes them nervous. It's hard for them to sleep at night."

Makayla doesn't reply.

"Bannon wants this guy real bad," Frank says. "Arrested and put away."

"I just—I don't know," Makayla says. "I mean, don't get me wrong. I did my twenty-eight weeks at the Academy. I know the law, and I'm prepared to enforce it. But"—she looks him in the eye—"I feel for him, sir. There's something very sad about it."

It's the lieutenant's turn to think her words over. He tugs on his ear, frowns. "There's no gray area here. We enforce the law." His face brightens into a smile. He pulls an item out of his pocket. "Ah, I almost forgot! This is for you. Let's just say I unofficially requisitioned it from someone's yellow Volvo."

Makayla accepts the silver dog whistle.

"You know how it works?" he asks, eyes mirthful.

Makayla's eyebrows go up.

"Dogs hear at a higher frequency than humans," he explains. "Some people, not too many, use these whistles as a training tool.

See here? This slide adjusts the pitch, You'll have to play around with it."

Makayla puts it to her mouth and blows. It produces a quiet hissing sound. She grins. "Why not, right?"

"Well, yeah. I suppose he had it in his glove compartment for a reason." Frank pauses, shifts tone. "It's a little fanatical, Brooklyn, if you ask me. Working on your day off. Are you sure?"

Makayla looks away. She sees volunteers gathering. Rangers talking. Some folks already heading up the trail. She feels the vibrant urgency of the mission.

"I'm sure," she says.

"You're a good ranger, Devaroix," Frank says. "Best of luck out there."

She returns to her big red Ford and rolls toward a little-used access road near Long Lake. She holds the dog whistle in her hand, rubbing it like a lucky rabbit's foot.

49

[NEW MORNING]

The color of Grace's ankle has become spectacular. A brilliant fusion of blue, green, red, and purple. Grace is impressed. The swelling has calmed down. She pokes at it with a pinkie, probes for tenderness. *Better*, she lies to herself. Maybe, a bit. Grace gulps down three Advil. Her morning ritual. She's been averaging ten Advil a day, and there's only four left.

She unwraps the bandage around her calf, feels discomfort in her ribs when she leans forward. A rank smell comes from the wound. The skin around it has blackened. It itches terribly. This wound is her biggest problem. If it becomes infected, Grace knows she'll get sick—maybe very sick. She pours the last of the hydrogen peroxide over the wound. Cleans it with a sterile pad. Running low on those, too. Reuses the old bandage to wrap gauze over the torn flesh, seals it with duct tape.

Sitka forages below. Nose to the ground, she sneezes, tail high, navigating the brambles. The dog's pace quickens; she pounces. Grace notices how the morning light changes everything. The wildflowers seem brighter, more plentiful. Have they always been here, and she's just now noticing? The sunlight ebbs in like a blood-orange tide, spilling color upon everything. The trees, the clouds, the rocks—all transform before her eyes, absorb the warmth from above. A volley of birdcalls fills the air. Grace feels her spirit awaken, like the petals of a flower unfolding. A new morning.

She hobbles on her walking stick down to the water, now practiced at the tottering shuffle. Sitka trots over, tail sweeping like a whisk broom, and gives a snuffle of contentment when Grace scratches her ears and face. "You're my best good girl," Grace tells the dog.

They both drink.

Grace isn't sure when she began talking to Sitka. She had always done it, of course, in small amounts: "Do you want a cookie?" or some other direction: "Sit, stay, lie down," that kind of thing. But this was different. This was the sharing of her innermost thoughts. She was thinking out loud . . . to the dog.

For her part, Sitka would tilt her head, perk up an ear, anything to hear better. After a while, Sitka accepted Grace's vocalizations of a kind of ambient earthsong, companionable sounds without real significance, like the babbling of a brook.

Grace began:

"Well, that's all there is to it. I'm not going to sleep another night like that. Today I'm going to improve my shelter. Home renovations," she says, grinning. "I'm going to start with a new mattress in the bedroom. Don't you think that's a good idea, Sitka?"

The dog does not object.

Grace looks to the sky, partially obscured by tree branches. She sits and confesses, "I was so sad last night, Sitka. I can't let that happen anymore. Look at this place. It's beautiful. We're here now. We've got to accept reality."

Sitka moves away, lies down in a patch of sunlight, still

listening. Grace laughs. "It looks like you already have! The thing to do now is wait—but I can't sit around and do nothing. I'll go bananas."

At the mention of that word, Grace feels the clenched fist of hunger in her belly. The energy bars are gone. Bugs, next. Maybe she should start scouting around. See what's on nature's menu.

So gross.

Grace spends much of that day gathering anything that will soften her bed. She works doggedly, with purpose. Graces saws at the branches of a hemlock, scraping her knuckles, covering her hands with sap and dirt. Hauls the boughs up, which is not easy in her condition. She spreads the curved branches with the ends stuck in the dirt, so there's a slight hump in the middle. Then she adds a mattress of moss and soft boughs.

By the end, she is exhausted. Her entire body throbs.

She lies down, breathes in the piney air, satisfied. And for that brief moment, Grace doesn't feel lost anymore.

50

[ASSASSIN]

While the boy still sleeps, John moves carefully about the camp. He removes the headlamp, returns it to its place. He ruminates on the compound bow—now hidden nearby, close at hand—and feels the coiled tension in his own body. He's adjusted the draw weight, tightened the limb bolts, tested the pull. It is powerful enough to shoot an arrow at 320 feet per second to pass straight through a bear. Puncture the lungs, devastate the heart. Important for the blood trail. The bow, and the hunter, are one. The weapon does not ask questions. The weapon is decisive. It simply does.

He seeks the clarity of the bow.

The certainty of the arrow.

The wisdom of the poet enters his mind: *Have little, gain much. Have much, become confused.*

He needs to simplify his life.

John has tried to disappear, strived to become empty, but this boy, asleep ten feet away, threatens to drag him back into the world. A groan comes from John's body. Old emotions, long sealed off, twist their way into his thoughts.

The boy's breathing changes. John knows at once he is awake. He boils water. Drops a tea bag in his one metal cup. Not enough dishware for guests. John runs both hands through his hair, massaging his scalp. He squeezes his eyes shut. He knows he's not right. The medicine never helped. Damaged in some irreparable way. His own parents turned against him, drove him to that clinic, forced him to meet with that self-important shrink, take all those pills. What a joke. The pills made it all so much worse. Never again.

The only salvation is in the here and now. So he concentrates on the boiling water. Watches the bubbles form. Vapors rise. He pours it into the cup, not spilling a drop. Allows the tea to seep. Estimates three minutes without once thinking of time. These are the simple, ordinary acts that serve to save his soul. He clings to this life raft in the roiling sea, too lost and alone to cry out, "Save me!"

The boy rouses, rises, sits on John's thinking rock. He shivers, coming awake, wearing John's big flannel for warmth.

John hands him the cup.

"Are we going today?" Carter asks.

"Drink," John says, motioning to the cup.

"Um, I'm scared about my sister. I need to—"

John snaps a stick. He is sinewy and strong. Taut as a wire. Drops both pieces at Carter's feet. "Who sent you?" he asks.

Carter lifts his head. "What?"

"Why did you come?" John says. "Do you think I'm dumb? Do you have a camera? Are you filming this?"

"Wait, what?" Carter says. "You brought me here, remember?"

"How would I even find your sister, anyway?" John asks. He waves an arm, gesturing violently. "She could be anywhere. How am I supposed to know?"

His eyes can't stay still. He never makes eye contact with Carter. Looks at his feet, his chest, or off in a different direction entirely.

"Okay," Carter says, trying to speak in a soothing voice. "If you could, maybe, just point me in the right direction. That's all I want."

"'Need little, want less,'" John says. "Lao Tzu. You come here to poison me with ideas. You bring the world here and lay it at my feet? Like it's some kind of prize?" He begins to pace. Five long strides, stops, turns, five strides back. "I'm supposed to give up my world to save yours? There are dangers out there you can't imagine." He withdraws his eight-inch knife. Picks up a stick from the ground. Starts carving. Peels the bark, smooths the surface, brings it to a sharp point that could pierce the skin. He violently pivots, lunges forward, drops to one knee, and stabs the stake into the ground. Gives it a final twist.

He starts pacing again.

Carter watches all this with a growing sense of horror, the big knife still in John's hand, an electricity coming off his body. It's as if he's become some other self. The alone man of the mountain. He seems twisted in a thousand different ways, filled with ghosts and demons. Carter shivers again, this time from a chill that has nothing to do with the cool, early-morning air.

John mutters words Carter can't discern at first. It comes out as garbled gibberish. It's as if John has forgotten that Carter is even here. After a while, the phrases become clear: "Be broken to be whole, twist to be straight, empty . . . to be full." He repeats them meditatively, over and over. "Broken to be whole . . . empty to be full."

Carter moves to lie back down. Retreats back into bed, the dark, safe place.

John suddenly wheels. His eyes flash fiercely: "Have I scared you? Is that it? Are you going to get the knife you stole? Didn't you think I'd miss it? Do you keep it next to you in the night? Is that your plan? To crawl out in the dark like a snake and slice my throat?"

Carter's heart freezes. His body, from head to toe, goes cold. He wants to speak. He wants to run. He can do neither. His throat feels constricted, as if he can't quite get enough air. His legs feel numb.

Is this how it feels, he wonders, *for an animal to be trapped in a cage?*

[WARMER]

Makayla holds a Dodger-blue hat in her hands. It's streaked with mud, water-stained, but not particularly misshapen. Which makes sense, since she found it on the fringe of the dank and waterlogged flatlands. It has not been here for long. She checks the hat for identification, a name scrawled in permanent marker, but no luck.

How did you get here? she inquires of the hat.

She knows the hat is Carter's, for dispatch has provided the search team with a description of the children's clothing, thanks to both parents' cooperation: the mother, clear-headed and detailed, driving up today with the help of a family friend; and the father from his hospital bed, lucid now, anxious and despairing. Makayla even has a picture on her phone. The children together, Carter wearing this very hat, blond hair flying out beneath it. Cute kid.

After some investigation, she finds the disorderly footprints in the bog. One person, traveling alone. Not a clear, steady pace. More the path expected of a drunken sailor, staggering home at night after the bars have shut down. She notes the direction and tracks them to firm ground. *Might have collapsed here*, she thinks, reading the smudged land. There's a spot near a willow where a second print enters the narrative. It is not a deep impression, but clear enough. A large boot. Makayla places her own much smaller foot beside it.

The air is still. A mosquito buzzes by the back of her neck. She tries to imagine the scene. The boy, alone, wandering through the bog. If he kept going, he could have made it to the access road and, eventually, Long Lake. She feels sure he didn't. She checks the ground for signs. Nothing. As if he disappeared. She finds a partial print that matches the big boot ten yards away, but headed in the direction of the willow and, presumably, the boy. But where did they go from here?

She ponders the stranger who lives hidden somewhere in these mountains. He must have found the boy. Makayla has no way of knowing if this is a good thing or a very bad thing. She's not optimistic. She spotted the man yesterday, alone. No boy. It's a puzzle, and too many pieces are still missing.

This wilderness park is an excellent place to disappear. But not forever. Makayla instinctively touches the holstered gun on her hip. Speaking calmly, she calls in to dispatch. Based on this new clue, the search will shift, take on new focus and momentum. She tucks the hat into her backpack and trudges on. There's messy work ahead. She must retrace the boy's steps through the mire. One made it out, but perhaps the second child, the girl, never did. Makayla braces herself for whatever she might find. Fearing that it could be the body of a thirteen-year-old girl named Grace.

Bogs are wonderful places—for insects and amphibians: frogs, salamanders, and newts. Cranes might nest here. Because bogs are acidic and nutrient-poor, perpetually in a state of arrested decay, only the heartiest plants thrive here. Makayla identifies pickerel weed, sphagnum moss (everywhere), holly, cranberry, blueberry, water lilies, loblolly pine, and other stunted evergreens. She notes varieties of insect-eating plants like sundew and Venus flytrap and, without pause, trudges on.

The path swerves and dips like a squiggly line, but leads her in a clear general direction. A sort of road *from* nowhere. It loosely fits the theory she outlined to Lieutenant Watkins in the morning. The map in her mind. Makayla doesn't know why the boy was alone—they split up for whatever reason—but she feels the chase growing warm. As always, she stops, calls, blows the silver whistle. Changes the frequency, blows again.

Her intention is fixed on retracing the boy's path, going to where he's been, in the hope it might lead Makayla to the girl. As she attains the higher elevation, she loses and rediscovers the trail a dozen times. She spies a broken twig, a squashed fern, the mark of a boot skidding in the mud, and her heart pumps with quiet triumph. Here the high timber, mostly fir and spruce and copses of white birch, creates a thick mesh whichever way she looks. Something catches her eye, a shape that doesn't belong. She picks up a water bottle, left standing on a rock next to a stream. His, surely. Makayla feels anxious excitement course through her body. Holding the bottle in her hands makes it all feel profoundly real. He stood here. The boy, Carter, drank exactly here. The searchers, behind her, will focus on the area below. Create a grid, go over it inch by inch. As they should. Makayla instead seeks where the boy once was, where he came from. For now, it leads up.

[ERRATICS]

Hours pass. Carter has to get up to use the bathroom. He tries to wait John out, but it is no use. Moving slowly, careful not to disturb John, Carter goes toward the pit in the ground. He says, "I just have to . . ." Scarcely above a whisper. The words catch in his throat. Afraid to make the wrong sound.

John calls, "Sprinkle a spoonful of lime in there when you're done. It keeps away the flies."

Carter looks at the plastic bag he noticed yesterday. So that's what it's for.

John welcomes him with food. "I have oats."

"Sure, thanks," Carter says.

He notes how John seems transformed, generously surrendering his seat on the rock to the boy. A new, softer John.

Carter decides to try a different tactic. See if he can keep John relaxed. Not be so high-strung. Carter tries a little conversation. He says, "I guess the chili you gave me that first day was a special treat?"

When was that? Carter wonders. *How long ago?* Not even two full days ago. He asks, "Do you know what day it is today?"

John opts to answer the first question. "Propane is precious. Cans of chili, rare. So yes, it was a treat. You needed something warm."

Carter nods. He eats quietly, head down, careful not to upset the man.

John hauls over a log. Not very big, but it serves as a second seat, which he now uses. "See that?" He gestures to the large rock. "Strange, right? Know what it's called?"

Carter knows a little bit about rocks. There are three kinds, basically: igneous, metamorphic, sedimentary. He doesn't venture a guess. Doesn't want to say the wrong thing.

"An erratic," the man says.

Carter almost doesn't reply. Still guarded. But John seems to expect some kind of human conversation. He's so strange and unpredictable. So Carter offers, "News to me."

"Look at it," John says. "It's a huge rock out here in the middle of nowhere, not attached to any formation you can see. Am I wrong?"

Carter sees that what John says is true. Eats the bland oats, wishes for milk, sugar. Still, it feels good in his belly.

John's thoughts are still on the erratics. "These mountains were formed, I've read, about five billion years ago. Give or take. But it's a constantly changing process. Nothing stays the same. Problem is, we live too fast to see it. We don't notice a thing. Here and gone. Blinded by the blur. But the rock remains. And it slowly, slowly changes."

"So how did it get here?" Carter asks.

"The last ice age happened about ten thousand years ago—"

"Wow," Carter says, eager to please.

John nods and almost, for the first time, smiles. "Powerful glaciers came in and carved up valleys. When the climate changed, the glaciers receded—meaning, the ice retreated—and when it did they randomly left these huge rocks behind. The erratics. Like these two. The sisters, I call 'em. You understand anything I'm talking about?"

Carter holds a thumb up, yes. But he's already thinking about his strips of red cloth. John has taken back the knife, but he never mentioned the cloth. Almost certainly never found it. Carter decides the next time John leaves him alone, he could leave behind strips of red cloth as he explores away from the camp. Little marks to help him find his way back—or maybe a way for someone to find him. Signals for the searchers leading the way to John's secret refuge.

It might work. It's a plan, at least.

"Do you think my father is looking for us?" he asks.

"Somebody, probably," John answers. His lips harden and turn downward.

"You worried about that?" Carter asks.

John looks at him, shakes his head, snorts. "They won't find us here."

Carter feels a chill in his bones. "I'll escape, you know."

"Good luck with that," John replies. "Remember, you're dead if I didn't come along. You're a walking ghost. Like me. Maybe we're both dead already. We walk the earth and leave no trace. It's the most noble thing a man can do."

"What do you mean?" Carter asks.

"Live, die, come, go, don't make it worse," John answers. "Leave the planet in peace."

Carter looks at the man for a long time. Hesitates, then utters the question: "What happened to you?"

John pauses, perhaps surprised by the directness of the question. He seems to be deciding on an answer. "War happened to me," he says. "The truth is, I'm an erratic, like those two rocks. I got left behind."

[WHISTLE]

Makayla does not want to haul butt all the way up to the summit. Not with this heavy pack on her back. She's carrying more than usual, unsure how long this journey might last. She's prepared to spend the night. Up she goes, for this is where the trail leads as she retraces the lost boy's wanderings. She wants to walk in his footsteps, toes pointing in opposite directions. *Isn't that how you get to know a person?* You walk a mile in their shoes, then multiply it by ten.

The ranger frequently pauses to pull out her map and compass. The tried-and-true, old-school method. She folds down the map, holding her right thumb at her present location, and orients it in the direction of travel. This way, she anticipates the terrain ahead. An advantage the boy, Carter, never enjoyed. Holding the clear compass over the map, she rotates the capsule to align the red orienting lines with the map meridians. Too many hikers depend entirely on their phone's GPS to direct them. It works great until they hit a dead zone or start using their phones as flashlights. The battery quickly loses its charge.

On the summit, Makayla unwraps a piece of raspberry-flavored gum. Chews it thoughtfully. She tries to imagine the scene as Carter might have perceived it. She stares out at the conical summit of Wolf's Snout, the sheer granite cliffs across the way, and the valley and flatlands below. When she looks upon Long

Lake glinting in the distance—beyond the bog through which she passed hours ago—Makayla feels certain the boy stood near this very spot. He saw the lake and must have thought: *That way.* Not knowing how improbably difficult it would be to get there. That old joke, told in a Maine accent: *You can't get there from here.* In the other direction lies Blood Mountain. On certain mornings, when the conditions are right, the sun drops down to rim the mountain with a bloodred glow. Thus, the name. She guesses that one of Carter's miscalculations came at this very spot, when he mistook Long Lake for Crater Lake, an error that took him farther in the wrong direction. Still, not a terrible strategy. Go to the lake, hope for the best. It gave him a destination. Maybe find somebody, something. Makayla is impressed. She is a former college athlete, an experienced trail runner in top physical condition. This long trek must have taken a tremendous toll on the boy, hiking without adequate food or sleep. The mind starts to do strange things under those conditions. Hikers begin to hallucinate, hear voices, lose all sense of the four fundamentals: water, shelter, warmth, food.

An hour later, she spies a cairn and a flash of yellow on the saddle point, or col, of the ridge. *Smart boy*, she thinks. Soon Makayla stands on that same spot, holds the wrapper in her hand, and takes a moment to absorb this sensation. The awesome, terrible beauty of this wilderness. She is flooded with hope, mixed with an undercurrent of dread.

Where is Grace? Amazing Grace?

Makayla puts the dog whistle to her lips, and blows. Adjusts the frequency, and blows again.

She calls, "Grace!"

Then she tries an ordinary whistle.

Turns and calls in all four directions.

Nothing happens.

Instinct causes her to linger longer than usual. She goes through the process again and again.

Until finally, like an answered prayer, she hears a bark.

[SLINGSHOT]

Carter observes John, amazed by his stillness. How he can do nothing—absolutely nothing—for hours at a time. Next chance he gets, Carter plans to escape. Until that point, he doesn't want to encounter John's dark side again.

Carter absently flicks a rock with his thumb. It is hard for him to sit still.

John half turns his head. Two squirrels skitter and quarrel on high, daredevils out on a limb. "You ever use a slingshot?" he asks.

"Maybe, um, not really, no," Carter stammers.

"Maybe, not really, no," John repeats. An amused smile crosses his face and quickly retreats, like a tourist on a dangerous street. He stands, scratches ferociously at his beard with both hands, and says, "Okay, then."

John goes to the tree, reaches his arm down a deep hole in the trunk. He pulls out the slingshot and a headlamp. He checks the light—it works—then thinks better of it. John returns the lamp to its storage place inside the tree.

"Come on," he says. "I know a spot. We're not going far."

Carter hesitates, once again confronted with a *different* John. He sees no alternative but to play along. They pass through the narrow gap between the two sisters. John turns sharply right, following along the side of the boulder, then bends into a small opening in the thicket, like a mouse squeezing through a crack in a wall. No wasted movement, no empty words: all efficiency. Carter follows, clumsily catching an ear in the prickers.

"See," John whispers. He gestures to a hollow where the grasses are bent down. Points to the marks on a tree where the bark's been scratched away. A smudged print, a pile of scat. "Bigfoot."

John turns and winks.

"Right." Carter forces a laugh. Suddenly John's his pal, and a comedian, too.

"Deer, actually," John says. "Antler rubbings."

They walk on, stepping carefully. John is particular about that. He watches Carter, signaling precisely where the boy should step. After one stern reprimand, Carter makes sure not to misstep. They come to a small clearing, a break in the trees, surrounded by thick understory and forest. John claws a small stone from the earth, not bigger than a marble. He lifts the sling from his back pocket. He wordlessly demonstrates the technique. Pulls the band back until it is taut, zings a blistering shot at a distant tree branch. Looks easy. He hands the weapon to Carter and talks him through the steps.

Carter understands at that moment how this is John's idea of training. He is teaching the boy how to survive in the wilderness. Not exactly what Carter has in mind. At the same time, the slingshot looks fierce. A skill worth having. Maybe it will come in handy down the road. After all, isn't that how David slayed Goliath? A rock to the skull?

Carter is willing to learn.

As instructed, Carter loads the rock into the center of the leather pouch, pinches it between the bone of his thumb and the knuckle of his index finger. He sets his feet at shoulders width.

He extends his left arm straight, elbow locked. Draws back the heavy elastic band.

"That band might be a little thick for you," John comments. "But it's good for hunting. There you go, nice and steady. Be sure to hold the fork even, not tilted or you'll miss your shot, maybe even hit your hand."

John impatiently takes the sling from Carter. "Draw the band back the same way every time," he says. "Like this. Right to your shoulder. Let your hand lightly touch your face. See? That's your mark. It never changes. You aim by adjusting your front hand. Up, down, left, right. Your trigger hand is the same every time."

His head drops down, his fingers separate, *thwonk*; the stone strikes its target.

It's Carter's turn. He aims for a tree about ten yards away— and hits it. Carter beams. He's enjoying this.

"Not terrible," John admits. "I like this spot for target practice. Plenty of practice ammo lying around. When I'm hunting for squirrels and rabbits, I use lead balls. Rocks are too irregular for consistent accuracy."

"Where do you get those?" Carter asks.

"Never mind that," John retorts.

One glare from John and Carter snaps back to reality. They aren't friends; they aren't buddies. John is a stick of dynamite; the slightest thing might set him off.

Carter shoots a half-dozen more stones, looking to John for approval, selecting smaller and more distant targets. John instructs him to exhale when he releases. "Back elbow up, don't let it drop like that," he reminds Carter. "It's all a nice, straight line."

The forest is quiet, save for the sounds of Carter's stones plunking against tree trucks or ripping through leaves. No one speaks.

"How long have you lived here?" Carter asks, attempting to break the awkward silence.

John doesn't answer.

"Does it get lonely?"

"No," John answers, so swiftly that it makes Carter wonder if it's true.

"When I was in that swamp," Carter confides, "I don't know. It got pretty crazy. It's scary to be alone."

John listens.

"You know what I mean?" Carter prods, irritated by John's silence.

John steps away. He takes his right elbow in his left hand and pulls it toward his left shoulder, loosening his back muscles. He reverses sides, does it again. He says, "Maybe that's who we really are. Those times we are alone. Our true selves." His voice husky and dry. He never looks at Carter. Instead seems to focus on some distant thing, a falling leaf, a passing cloud, anywhere but here. His mind ten thousand miles away. "To be honest, I feel more lonesome when I'm in a crowd."

"But you can't live here forever," Carter says. "You need help. Doctors and stuff, in case you get sick."

"Doctors," John grumbles. "It's better for everyone this way."

"You need *things*, too," Carter points out. "Batteries and food and clothes. No one can exist out here all alone."

John nods, looks away. Just when it seems like the conversation has concluded, he says, "I'm just trying to live as far from people as I can."

Carter aims and hits a distant target—high up on the slender branch of a dead ash tree.

"I have caches of supplies squirreled away in different parts of these mountains," John says with a touch of pride. "If there's trouble, I'll be all right. It's not all slingshots, I'll tell you that."

"What kind of trouble?" Carter asks.

"Shhh," John hushes. He points to a squirrel that has paused on a tree trunk. "Take the shot."

Carter shakes his head. He won't do it.

John teases, "You're just not hungry enough."

"Guess not," Carter says.

"Not yet," John states.

Carter hands the weapon back to John. The lesson has concluded. He asks, "Don't you ever miss it? All the cool stuff?"

"Cool stuff?" John repeats. There's new passion in his voice. A trace of bitterness, too. "That's all anyone wants. More and more stuff. The road to happiness. You think that's the *answer*? It's the *problem*. People become free not by fulfilling their desires, but by eliminating them."

"Okay, but," Carter says, "some things make life better."

"Like what?" John asks.

"Like, I don't know, computers," Carter offers.

"Computers? That's why I got off the grid in the first place." John looks up to the sky, rubs the back of his neck, his mouth drawn into a grimace. "The government already knows too much about us. Watching, spying, eavesdropping. Satellites, drones, cameras everywhere. Probably watching us right now."

A wind kicks up, swirls around them. Carter feels the cold creep under his shirt. "What about winter?"

"Winter gives me focus," John replies. "Like the squirrels, I'll prepare, stock up, get fat. I've got a little cave all picked out. Winter is the magic time. You'll see. A stillness comes to this place. Not a bug, not hardly a bird."

Carter heard it. *You'll see.* Was that a slip? Did John really expect Carter to stay? Is that what's been going on here? John is training him for survival?

"Sounds miserable," Carter says.

"No," John replies. "It's purifying. I love the suffering. It's when I feel most alive."

And again says, "You'll see."

"You think I'm crazy, don't you?" John says to Carter. It is an accusation, not a question. And like that, the mood shifts.

55

[COME]

Sitka feels the warm rays on her back as she makes her daily inspection of the sun-dappled forest. She noses through ferns and deadfall the way an avid reader turns the pages of a book. Pausing, considering, moving forward but also, sometimes, turning back. The girl, Grace, dozes in her regular spot against the wall, beneath the overhang. She's not herself, fatigued and feverish. A faint sound reaches Sitka's ears. She stops, waits, hears it again, louder this time.

It is a sound ingrained into her through hours and days and weeks of training. A noise she *knows*. It calls to her, commands her: *Come*.

She hurries to the girl, pokes Grace with her nose. Whimpers, prods again. Grace covers her head with the Mylar blanket.

Sitka barks twice, nudges again.

Grace rubs her eyes, woozily drags herself awake. Her face feels warm. The dog stands, staring at her, whining persistently.

"What?" Grace asks.

Sitka taps Grace with a paw as if to say, *Come on, it's time*.

Grace sees that Sitka is wildly excited. Tail thumping emphatically. Body trembling, torn by conflicting desires. The dog scampers a few feet, almost prancing, comes back, barks in Grace's face.

"Oh, sweetie, I'm sorry," Grace says. "But I don't understand." She lies back down.

Then thinks: *Wait.*

A feeling stirs in her heart. Like a jolt of electricity. *Could it be?* Grace reaches for the backpack, finds the whistle, blows using the side of her mouth that's not cracked and swollen.

She scrambles to her feet.

Listens, yearns, hopes, blows again.

She doesn't hear a thing.

But Sitka persists, runs away again, returns with a wild urgency in her eyes.

"What do you want?" Grace asks again. She becomes newly aware of her position beside the rock wall, beneath the overhang, and realizes it is almost impossible for her to hear any sound originating from above. Or, even worse, for any searchers to hear her.

She looks at Sitka—the dog is bursting with repressed energy—and asks: "Do you smell something? Hear something?"

Sitka can't reply. Her mouth opens and shuts, ears twitching.

Grace gestures, "Okay then. Go." Sitka stays, confused. Grace places her hands gently on the sides of the dog's head. Says softly, "I love you. It's okay. Go, find it." Now she stands tall and dramatically points. In the tone of command, she orders, "Go, Sitka. Go now!"

It is a directional gesture the dog understands, combined with the high-pitched whistle she well remembers. Sitka turns and runs. She follows the trail blazed by the boy just two and a half days before. The scent trail is faint, but the whistle grows louder.

Then . . . silent.

Sitka barks. She is not yet to the hardscrabble scree. The girl, Grace, alone below. Sitka lifts her snout to the air, vacuums in a cacophony of odors. Deer and pine and wintergreen, vole and rain and decay . . . and raspberry-flavored something. The dog takes the slope in leaps and bounds and suddenly stiffens.

Sitka stares at a tall, dark woman in a wide-rimmed hat. It is not the man after all. Sitka backs up a step, barks once, twice, three times. The figure kneels, her body softens, shows her straight white teeth. "Are you alone out here? Come, dog," the woman says. And then remembers, "Sitka."

Sitka woofs again. Not a threat. An invitation. She runs down the hill about fifteen feet. Runs back up again, front paws stretched out, rump high, tail up beseechingly.

Makayla shouts, "Grace!"

No answer.

She cautiously follows the dog down the long slippery slope, careful not to fall, awkward with her heavy pack, yet at the same time jumping out of her skin with excitement. Sitka pauses, looks back, imploring the young woman in the wide-rimmed hat to hurry along. The ranger cups a hand around her mouth, gives another full-throated scream. "Grace? Grace Taylor! Can you hear me?"

56

[DAMAGE]

John and Carter are back at camp, eating cold rice. They share a bowl of fresh blackberries. John calls it his daily "harvest."

Out of the blue, John presses the question again: "I'm crazy, right? Is that what you think?"

To Carter, John's question feels like a minefield. He isn't sure how to respond, knows there is no good answer. Before he can tiptoe through a reply, John continues:

"I'm not the crazy one." John jabs a finger in the air. It darts closer to Carter's face. The boy leans away. "You think I'm lonely? Like I'm missing out on the wonders of the world?"

Scary John is back.

"I'm not sick. I don't need doctors. You know what's sick? Society! The cruel, ugly, violent world out there! I reject it. I threw it all away." He waves an arm. "And now you want me to go crawling back on my hands and knees?"

"No, John, I'm not saying that," Carter says.

"I walk the righteous path," John claims. "I reject your world. I regulate my life. I keep life simple, clean, orderly. Lao Tzu: 'Those with less become content, those with more become confused.'"

"I don't understand," Carter says.

John brushes off the comment. He's back to pacing again, the long strides of a tall, lean man. "I'm not going, I'm not going," he repeats vehemently. "People pound me, mash me, probe me with questions. They tell me how to act, what to feel, then hand me a bottle of pills and tell me to swallow."

He stalks, and walks, and pivots to stare at Carter. Wide-eyed but blind. His muscles taut, high-strung. Truly *wired*. Like before, he's there and he's not there. And like before, Carter wishes to make himself small. John concludes, "The world is not made for people like us."

Us? Carter thinks.

"They will drop the bomb. They've already done it, and they'll do it again—blow the whole thing up. It's too dangerous out there, Carter," John says, almost pleading. "This, right here, is the last true place left. I can't let you go."

Desperate, Carter pleads, "You're wrong, John. I have a home. I have a family!"

The bearded man angrily steps toward Carter, hands balled into fists, the veins in his arms turned dark blue. Carter flinches, covers his head with his arms. And as if waking from a daze, the soldier stops. Blinks, spits in disgust, turns away. He does not speak. John crawls into the depths of his soul, where the demons play their wicked games, and sojourns in that shadowy place for the remainder of the night.

Mumbling indecipherably.

Carter makes a promise to himself.

Tonight, he will stay awake. He will wait John out. And then, in the dark, he will slip away.

57

[HERE]

Moments after Sitka departs, Grace sees a lone black bear ambling lazily through a copse below. It is twenty-five yards away. A distance that a bear can cover, if sufficiently motivated, in less than three seconds. The powerful animal vectors in a diagonal from near left to far center, as if cutting through Grace's backyard. It pauses to chew on a berry or flower, emits a gruff sound, and swivels its head to gaze in Grace's direction.

Grace stands perfectly still, unsure if the bear sees her, motionless against a dark gray backdrop. The bear is smaller than she imagined, though Grace does not doubt its strength. She remains calm. It all feels, to Grace, strangely . . . not terrifying. She is glad Sitka's not here to raise a ruckus. That would have made everything worse. No, this is a private moment between her and nature, when the wall between them temporarily crumbles. Sky and earth, distant star to deep-delving root, Grace and black bear, fused in a sort of communion.

Bored or just indifferent, the bear saunters away, deeper into the forest. *Becomes* the dark forest. The wild, the dangerous, the fanged and clawed and forbidding. The beast in the garden.

Moments later comes the cry of a human voice from above: "Grace? Grace Taylor! Can you hear me?"

A whistle cuts through the air, loud and clear.

"Here!" Grace shouts. "I'M RIGHT HERE!"

Grace hobbles forward on two bad legs. One with a deep, infected gash in the right calf; the other with an ankle that has become a swollen knot of pain. A stabbing, ever-present ache in her ribs. Yet she very nearly skips toward the direction of the voice.

Sitka appears, runs to the girl, mouth open, tongue out, triumphant. Leaps up to Grace and nearly knocks her back. "You did it!" Grace tells Sitka, stroking her neck and head. "Oh, my best good girl, my best good girl!" A woman follows. She wears a green uniform, has free-flowing black hair, and the biggest smile Grace has ever seen.

"Grace? I'm Ranger Devaroix." The woman introduces herself, giving a little wave. She unbuckles the belt of her pack, sets it on the ground. "We've been looking for you."

The ranger steps toward Grace and extends a hand. Grace staggers forward and sinks into the woman's arms—sobbing, wiping away tears, hiccupping, laughing, sniffling—swept away by a torrent of pent-up emotion.

They hug without words for a long time.

The girl smells of earth and pine and perspiration, the ranger of raspberry gum with a hint of maple syrup.

The ranger reaches for her radio. "Dispatch, this is Devaroix." Her voice catches, choked with feeling. "I am in contact with the female subject. Her condition appears fair. No further resources needed at this time. I will contact you again after a full patient assessment. But, yes, good news. Very good news."

Grace squeezes tight upon hearing those words, all the fear

and anxiety and relief spilling out. It feels so good to be held. To cry. To know she'll be going home. To again see her mother, her father, her brother. She looks up into the ranger's astonishing steel-gray eyes and says, "I saw a bear."

[AMAZING]

W here's Carter? Did he send you? Is he okay?" Grace asks in rapid-fire succession. The ranger's face provides the answers before she can even open her mouth. Sitka circles around them, watching closely.

Makayla gently takes Grace by the shoulders, looks into her eyes. "Grace, listen to me," the ranger says. Her voice is calm and clear. "I believe your brother is still out there—"

Grace shakes her head, disbelieving. "He can't be! Carter left—what?—two, three days ago. It's not possible."

"Grace," Makayla interrupts. "I believe that he's safe. And I promise you—I promise—that we will not stop looking until we find him."

The girl rubs her eyes, sags with sudden weariness. The dog is at her side. Grace absently touches Sitka, strokes her head, runs her fingers through Sitka's silky ears.

"Grace, we'll talk all about it. I need to know everything that happened. But right now, there are things we need to do." She pauses, "You must be hungry."

"You have food? With you?" Grace asks.

"I do," Makayla answers. "I've been carrying it around just for you. But here, let's sit. While you eat, I'd like to examine your wounds, make sure you're okay, clean you up a little bit."

Makayla needs to complete a thorough patient assessment,

including a set of vitals: pulse, blood pressure, respiration, etcetera. A full head-to-toe exam. At the same time, since the subject appears to be in no imminent danger, the ranger eases into the work. She gives Grace space to enjoy this moment of rescue. Makayla unzips her pack, pulls out a medical kit—and two dazzlingly bright clementine oranges. She deftly peels one, tucking the rinds into the pack's side pocket. Hands one to Grace. "Eat slowly," Makayla advises.

The ranger helps Grace hobble back to her usual spot, beside the pine-bough bed and pile of stones. Grace lowers to a seated position, wincing as she does, her back against the rock wall.

Miraculously, a blue Gatorade bottle appears.

"My favorite," Grace says.

Makayla smiles. "That's what your mother told us."

Grace drinks, burps softly, excuses herself, giggles. "You talked to my mother?"

"I did not," Makayla answers. "But our people did."

"What about my dad?" Grace asks.

"He's worried about you," Makayla answers. She decides to save that story for later. Working calmly, Makayla gives Grace a complete examination, palpating every inch of the patient's body. Cleans and dresses her wounds, splints the ankle, wraps the ribs, checks Grace's eyes, ears, nose, and throat. Gives her two Advil. "Take two of these and call me in the morning," Makayla jokes.

Grace smiles. "You're good at this. Thank you."

Makayla touches the front rim of her hat, nods, slightly embarrassed. "Overall, I'd say you've held up remarkably well. But what happened? It looks like you were in a motorcycle accident."

Grace puts a finger straight up. "I fell."

"From there?" Makayla tilts her head back, hands on her lower back. "Oh my. I guess you really are Amazing Grace after all." She rummages around in her pack. Pulls out clean, freshly laundered clothes. Wool sweatpants, warm socks, a wool hat, shirt, and fleece. "I thought maybe . . ."

Grace accepts the offering of clothes. She brings the items to her face and breathes deep. "Heaven," she says. "Thank you so much."

"My pleasure," Makayla responds. "Listen, I'm going to walk to that spot right there and make a call. There's a lot of people— and I mean *a lot* of people—who've been worried about you and your brother. Let me catch them up while you get dressed." She snaps her fingers, eyes twinkling. "I forgot something!" Makayla takes out a plastic bag. Unwraps it. Sitka steps up, tail swishing, intently curious. "Yes, that's right, this is for you," Makayla says, and hands Sitka a rawhide bone. The dog would laugh out loud if she could. But instead, she snatches the treat in her mouth, pads away about ten yards, and begins working on it.

Ten minutes later, the ranger sits down beside Grace, who looks revived in fresh, clean clothing. Makayla produces a new surprise from her bag—a hairbrush. She says with a light laugh, "Do you mind if I . . . ?"

While Makayla brushes the knots out of Grace's hair, she says, "Grace, I need to know everything."

Grace recounts every detail. Getting lost, falling, Carter's decision to go for help.

"Did you ever see a man?" Makayla asks.

Grace turns to look at Makayla, baffled. "A man? Here?

No, no." She pauses, "Was I supposed to?" And then, piecing it together, asks, "Is this about Carter?"

"I don't know," Makayla answers. "But maybe, yes. I think so."

Grace is suspicious. "What kind of man?" Her eyes again become red-rimmed, wet as river stones.

"Shhh," Makayla says. She takes Grace's head in her hand, inclines it toward her shoulder. Grace submits, tears roll down. "Just try to stay calm for now," the ranger says. "You've been through so much."

"You have to find him," Grace says, shuddering, her voice muffled in Makayla's shoulder.

"I will," the ranger replies. "I will."

After a while, Makayla stands, surveys the scene, taking it all in. She's impressed that Grace has endured so well. "We still have a few items on our agenda."

Graces looks up, curious.

"Have you ever been in a helicopter?"

She explains that they have a couple of choices. Because of the lateness of the day, and the foggy weather conditions, they felt it might be best to extract Grace—that is, take her off the mountain—in the morning. "But only if that's all right with you," Makayla quickly states. "A team can carry you down tonight. They have big flashlights and it would be very safe."

"Or?" Grace says.

"Or," Makayla says. "We spend one more night here, together. Physically, I believe you're okay for now. The damage has been done. It's not going to get any worse by waiting another day. I have a lightweight tent and a sleeping bag for you. And plenty more food."

Grace's eyebrows lift. "More food?"

"Bread, peanut butter, cheese, fruit," Makayla says.

"Seriously?"

"We rangers don't mess around," Makayla replies. "If you give me a few minutes, I can get myself organized. I'm thinking"—she points—"right here for the fire."

"Fire? Really?" Grace is thrilled.

And that is how the night passes, in the chill blue-black of shadow and dusk. A small fire turns the rock wall a luminous orange. Sitka sprawled beside it, content and warm.

Grace finishes the night by polishing off a bag of M&M's. She yawns, arches her back, and wearily snuggles in the coziest, warmest sleeping bag the world has ever seen. "Are you sure?" Grace asks.

Makayla rests on her own pine-bough bed, wearing thick socks and a spare heating blanket that Grace's condition didn't require. "I'm so sure," she answers.

It is quiet, except for a few night noises. The call of a coyote. An owl's hoot. Grace points. "Do you see that tree there, the one where the branches stick straight out?"

"Yeah," the ranger says.

"Do you know the name of it?"

But before Makayla can answer, Grace yawns again and drifts away. She sinks into her best night's sleep in days.

[THE BOY]

Carter lies awake, listening.

John is out there, methodically whittling down a piece of wood. It is dark, and there's a chill to the air. It feels thick and wet. Another fog rolls over the mountains.

The man pushes aside the tarp flap, appears at the narrow entranceway. He's on his knees, wearing only sweats and a thin T-shirt. He leans in on one hand, an arm's length away. His presence charges the air, emits a pulse of threat.

"There was a boy," John begins. His voice low and intense.

Carter turns away, too uneasy to look at John's face. It doesn't matter. John has a story to tell.

"About your age," he continues. "Skinny, like you."

John stops, scratches a cut on his right forearm.

"Over there?" Carter asks.

Another silence. Slow breathing. "Yeah, over there," John says. "A village kid I got to know."

Carter decides that he can't ignore John, whose head is now poking into his sleeping area. He asks, "What was he like?"

"I used to watch him through the night-vision goggles, you know. I'd glass the village, code orange every single day, see what's what."

"I don't—" Carter says, confused.

"Marine on high alert," John replies. "Anyway, we never

talked. Two different worlds. And this boy—I felt like I got to know him a little bit. Just from watching. Jet-black hair, about your length. He liked to kick around a ball with the same three friends. Always on the move. Mischievous. Eyes, you know, looking everywhere all the time. But one late afternoon, *boom*, land mine. Out of luck. IEDs, we called them. Improvised explosive devices. Took off his leg. He died on the street, too shocked to even scream."

"Oh" comes out of Carter, pushes past his lips without thought, a sound a person might make after getting punched in the gut. And then, lamely, "I'm sorry. That must have been horrible."

"Yes," John replies. "War. Funny thing is, that IED was never meant for him. Isn't that something when you think about it? They blew up their own kid." He laughs a little, a choking sound.

Carter hears John sit back, the rustling of his legs, a body trying to get itself comfortable. He hears, also, a soft sob—a sadness that could turn the stars blue. John rubs his hands together, claps them once, resettles himself. Carter cranes his neck to watch.

John's voice seems to come from some other place, the way the wind arrives from far off. Some other time, some other world. "When I was there, I had a rifle in my hands all the time. I didn't want to ever let it go. It was just always there, you know? Like a security blanket, I suppose. After deployment, when they sent me home, I didn't know what to do with my hands anymore. Isn't that strange? For weeks, I just didn't know where to put my hands. In my pockets? Folded across my chest? Hanging at my sides like slabs of meat?

"Over there, it's all you think about. Getting to the next minute. The one right in front of you. That's it. We were up in this mountain outpost. The most terrifying place I've ever been. One night, in the desert cold, things got bad. We took on sniper fire. Pinned down, waiting for support. I was stranded up there with one other guy, Emerson, and he bled out in my arms. He just trickled away."

John gives a delicate gesture. Reaches out with two fingers, gently lowers them. "I closed Emerson's eyelids and said good-bye."

Carter turns to his side, rises on his right elbow. John sits slumped, staring at the ground. A broken man. He says to the boy, to the wind, to the mountain itself, "I often wonder who died out there, and who came home."

In the aftermath of that story, Carter promises himself that he will not cry. Not here, not now, not in front of his captor. A promise he almost keeps.

The bearded man raises his head, stares at the boy. This time, he seems to see him: Carter Taylor, eleven years old, desperate to find a way home.

"We're stronger together," John finally says. "I'm doing you a favor."

He winks.

Carter sinks down to his back. Closes his eyes. Tries hard not to react, refuses to surrender. There's no point trying to bargain. Carter is sure his words would never reach the fractured inner core of John's reality.

He's more lost than me, Carter realizes.

He clutches the balled-up shreds of cloth in his fist. Knows he's leaving before the morning light.

DAY 6

[ESCAPE]

Carter sees that John has adapted to his surroundings. He's become nocturnal, like many creatures of the forest. Avoids the daylight. Safer that way. So Carter feigns sleep, holds himself still, and waits for John to shut his eyes. When the rain persists, John grumblingly goes off, disappears to some near supply area, and returns to assemble a primitive shelter with sticks, stakes, and tarp. Carter observes the outline of John's movements in the dark. John expertly sets up the shelter five feet from the entranceway to Carter's cozy, dry sleeping area.

Carter won't attempt an escape until his captor is safely asleep. Carter bites his lip, squeezes his hands into fists, tries to stay awake, and fails spectacularly. Eyelids flutter closed. Hours later, he awakens to a sound. A small animal scurries away. Still dark, but the unbright light of crepuscular dawn draws near. Heart thumping, furious with himself, Carter strains to listen. He glimpses the bottom of John's foot, clad in a thick gray sock, motionless at the tent's edge.

Carter rolls to his side, eases to all fours, arches his back, and slinks like a cat into the open. The drizzle dampens the air. He can hear the faint murmur of fine water drops on the canopy's moist leaves and needles. He lifts his empty boots from the ground, carefully navigates the space around John's tent. Carter steps to the tree, reaches into the hole—his heart stops when the headlamp makes a muffled clink—he stands and waits, his hand in the cookie jar—until he is sure that John has not stirred. Improvising, Carter pauses at the kitchen area. The small knife lit by moonlight. Carter pockets it and steals away on silent stocking feet.

Beyond the crack between the rocks, Carter sharply veers right, then ducks under the opening that John showed him the day before. He stands frozen, listens, turns on the headlamp. Carter struggles to stay calm, cool, collected. Every instinct in his body urges him to run. He steps, stumbles, catches himself. Still unshod, his dangling boots thump against the base of a tree.

He doesn't wait.

He's up and gone, eyes trained on the ground, moving swiftly now across a carpet of pine needles. Three minutes later, he yanks on his boots, laces them tight. Carter ties a scrap of red cloth at knee level, rises to full height. He fears getting hopelessly lost. He can't allow that disaster to occur again. If things go bad, like down in that bog, he needs to be able to find his way back. When John discovers the red cloth—and he eventually will—Carter hopes to be long gone. Leaving so close to dawn was not the plan, but he couldn't stay another day. John was too erratic, too damaged. Carter doesn't want to be there the next time John loses it.

The cold, damp air cuts through the layers of his clothing. The rocks and roots are slippery. After a time, Carter turns off the headlamp. He selects a way through the sparse understory of sapling and bush. Walks swiftly, covers ground, pauses only to tie a red scrap to a twig. It's full light when Carter comes to a clearing. Miraculously, he spies a helicopter in the distance, hovering above the ground. Carter waves his knife in a sweeping arc over his head, jumps up and down, wills the copter pilot to look his way.

Carter is afraid to scream, and the distance is too great for the pilot to hear anyway.

I'm here, he thinks. *Find me, I'm right here.*

The copter tilts away, shrinks into the horizon. He watches it grow smaller, farther away, a black speck, gone.

The rain stops.

Carter keeps going.

At least now, he has a direction, a fixed point. He's headed for the spot where that helicopter just hovered.

Behind him, padding silently, the hunter follows.

[GUESTS]

Grace rises to find Ranger Devaroix sitting with Sitka by a small, toasty fire. Grace rubs the sleep from her eyes.

"Good morning. You slept well," Makayla observes.

Grace smiles, loosens her stiff body with small, gentle twists. If she tries to do too much, the pain comes shrieking back. Her ankle refuses to improve, though the splint helps. She feels clean and rested. Her spirits are high.

"What's for breakfast?" Grace asks, ravenous.

"I hope you don't mind, but I ordered in," Makayla replies. "Should be arriving any minute."

Grace laughs at the joke, hobbling over on the walking stick. "I know Domino's delivers to weird places, but I'm not that gullible."

Makayla grins and says, "Oh, ye of little faith." She tends to the fire with a stick. "I made peppermint tea. Would you like a cup?"

"Yum," Grace replies.

Twenty minutes later, Sitka rises, gives a low, warning woof. She lopes forward to investigate. "It's okay, girl, no worries," Makayla says in a soothing voice. She hustles to Sitka's side, touches her back, waves to someone out of sight.

A moment later, three rangers drop down from the path. Two men and a woman. The mustached, red-haired man, arriving first, cheerfully asks, "Did somebody order a toasted poppy seed bagel with cream cheese?" He holds up a brown bag.

"Oh wow, you weren't kidding!" Grace gushes.

"Rangers never kid," Makayla deadpans. Then, to her fellow rangers, "Thanks, you guys are the best. You must have gotten an early start this morning."

"Couldn't wait," says one of the rangers, Megan, smiling warmly at Grace.

They make introductions all around.

The last ranger, Smitty, short and solid as a vending machine, produces a bag of dog biscuits from his side pocket. Sitka can't believe her good fortune. She wolfs down the treats with astonishing speed. Smitty looks from Makayla to Grace, "So, Grace. Are you ready for this?"

Confused, Grace looks to Makayla for answers.

Makayla explains, "We plan to fly you out by helicopter. The chopper will bring you directly to County General, where doctors and nurses can attend to your injuries, make sure everything's okay from a medical standpoint. I'm sure you'll be fine, though my guess is you might need at least a walking boot on that ankle. Possibly surgery. Depends if your injury is musculature or skeletal. Only X-rays can help determine that." She pauses, saving the best for last. "Your parents will be waiting for you."

Grace's lower lip trembles, and she nods at Makayla. The thought of her parents nearly overwhelms her. Now that it's over, her defenses down, Grace feels raw and emotional.

"The challenge, however, is finding a good spot for an extraction," Makayla continues.

"Nothing is ever simple out here," the red-haired ranger, Liam, explains.

Smitty chimes in, grinning. "That's why they asked me to come. I'm the muscle."

The other rangers roll their eyes, chuckling.

"How far away is it, Megan?" Makayla asks the broad-shouldered, blond ranger.

"A good twenty-minute walk over rough ground," Megan estimates. She shifts her gaze to Grace. "I won't lie to you, Grace. It's not a comfortable trip in the basket. Nobody loves it."

Grace listens as they detail the procedure. She'll be strapped, quite tightly, into a stretcher known as a Stokes basket. It has aluminum railings on all sides to keep her from spilling out. The rangers will carry her to the extraction point where she'll be hoisted up by a cable to a hovering helicopter.

"That's kind of scary," Grace observes.

"It kind of is," Liam agrees, smiling. "Again, Grace. The hike won't be a lot of fun for you. But I do think you'll enjoy the helicopter. You're not afraid of heights, are you?"

"I suspect she's not afraid of anything," Megan says, winking good-naturedly at Grace.

Grace turns to Makayla. "You've all done this before?"

"Many times," Makayla assures her. "We will take good care of you, I promise."

Grace puts her arm around Sitka. "What about . . . ?"

Smitty answers, "I've brought a leash—and a *lot* more biscuits. I'll walk her down myself. We'll take good care of Sitka until someone can pick her up."

Liam and Megan prepare the basket, begin fiddling with straps.

Grace touches Makayla's arm in alarm. "Right now?"

Makayla sees something in Grace's face. She stands, says to the other rangers, "Let's give Grace a few minutes alone. She's been here in this location for almost four full days. Besides, I've got to gather up my gear."

Megan looks around, glances at Grace's pine-bough bed, admires the forest view, "You picked a pretty spot. I like what you've done with it."

They give Grace time by herself.

Grace hop-limps to her usual place, the area where she spent most of the past days. Standing on one leg, with two hands clasped on the walking stick, she lowers herself to the ground. Grace wants to remember everything. The early-morning rain has stopped. The verdant forest feels wet and fresh and drippy and impossibly green. She closes her eyes, breathes deeply, listens intently.

Grace opens her eyes again. Her lips move. She hears herself say, soft as a prayer, "Thank you." It surprises Grace to hear her own voice filled with so much gratefulness, and in that moment her heart fractures a little bit—a thin line from which shines forth a beam of pure love. Grace understands she will never be the same. It is the forest's gift to its gentle visitor, bestowed by ancient trees and excellent birds. Grace hadn't realized until that moment exactly how she felt. But it was true. This place, these memories, the towering trees she cannot name. The wildflowers seemingly everywhere once she opened her eyes to notice them. The wandering black bear, snorting in the brambles, utterly indifferent to her.

The rangers stand chatting in a loose group. Makayla glances over, keeping a sharp eye on the girl.

Grace nods. She's ready. Makayla comes over.

"Will you miss it?" she asks.

"I think so, yes."

"Would you like me to take a picture?" Makayla offers. "There's no Wi-Fi, but my phone works."

"No, that's all right," Grace answers. She points to her head. "I just did."

"I understand," Makayla answers.

"Are you coming with us?" Grace asks.

"I'll help get you to the extraction point," Makayla replies. "See you off okay. But you know I'm not leaving this mountain." She squeezes Grace's hand. "We'll find him, Grace. We're close. I can feel it."

[EXTRACTION]

Despite the determined efforts of four rangers, Grace does not enjoy being jostled in the Stokes basket. The straps are tight and extremely uncomfortable. She toggles on the edge of nausea with each step, suffering in silence, eyes squeezed shut.

"The worst is over," Makayla finally announces as they set her on the ground.

"Now, the fun part," Smitty says. He's holding Sitka by a green leash. Sitka sniffs Grace's face, licks her mouth, her sore and still swollen lower lip. Grace senses the dog's apprehension. "It's okay, Sitka." Smitty steps back, gently tugs the dog away. Megan and Liam get to work, attaching four cables to a central anchor point above the basket. They labor diligently, with utmost seriousness, checking and double-checking their work.

Liam explains, "When the helicopter arrives, it will lower a cable. This is where we'll secure the tag line. Keep your hands in, don't try to reach out. Let the rangers in the chopper do the work. Just enjoy the ride."

"You'll do fine," Makayla says, kneeling by Grace's side.

Grace works up a smile, heart beating a hundred miles a minute. Soon the copter arrives, and up she rises, soaring into the sky like some sort of human balloon filled with helium. She is afraid to turn her head. Afraid to wiggle a toe. She stares straight up as the helicopter draws her closer. It is very loud.

Grace cries, "Thank you!" but the chopper's roar drowns out the words. The whirling blades scatter them over the park, unheard.

Makayla stands watching, hands on her hips. It all goes smoothly. Once Grace is secured, the copter hovers in place an extra few seconds. Makayla waves. The helicopter rises, tilts away, slides into the distance. Across the valley, on the next ridge, Makayla notices a momentary glint of light. One flash, the sun's rays bouncing off something, then gone. It lasts less than a second. But it is enough. Makayla fixes the location in her mind.

She knows where she's headed next.

Makayla must make a decision. Smitty is already headed in the direction of a spur trail, which will hook up with the main trail, and ultimately lead him and the dog back to the trailhead. Just ninety minute's distance to the main trail . . . when an experienced hiker knows the way. Megan and Liam stand aside, perhaps waiting to confer with Makayla before making their next move.

"Aren't you headed down?" Liam asks.

"What? Oh, um, I left my truck"—Makayla points northwest—"out by Long Lake." She pauses, conflicted. "And honestly, I'm still thinking about Carter, the boy. I want to check something out."

"Would you like company?" Megan asks.

"No, no, I'm good," Makayla says. She looks across the way, to where she saw that fleeting glimpse of light reflected from the trees. She wavers, uncertain. Makayla realizes that communication and trust are at the bedrock of all ranger activities. They depend on each other. No secrets. She admits, "I may have seen something. Probably my imagination."

Makayla tells her fellow rangers about the mountain man she saw the previous day. "I want to go after this alone," she says.

Megan asks, "And why is that a good idea?"

"I'm concerned that he might be on edge," Makayla replies. "If we appear in numbers, it could set him off. If I'm right, he won't respond well if he feels threatened. We come in wrong, it could become dangerous. He's already seen me. I believe our best chances for a safe encounter will be if I'm alone."

Megan looks to Liam, who says, "We'll remain nearby and provide backup. Keep us informed of your location. Just give us a call and we'll get there. Deal?"

It's agreed.

Megan says, "Great work, Makayla. Stay safe. We've got your back."

"Thanks," Makayla says. "I appreciate that. You guys are the best."

Liam touches the brim of his hat with two fingers, inclines his head. Makayla turns and walks away.

Makayla thinks of the boy, and of the man she saw yesterday. The search zone is tightening. Local police are seeking an arrest. She wants to be the first officer to find them. This could be a dangerous situation. She'll need to handle it with supreme care. The wrong approach—too aggressive—and things could turn bad.

A call comes in. "This is Devaroix," she answers.

"Brooklyn, this is your doughnut-stuffed lieutenant," Frank Watkins says. "I hear the package is on its way."

Makayla breaks into a smile. *The package.* "Yeah, we wrapped her up pretty tight."

"You did good out there," he says.

"Thank you, sir."

"Tell me. Did the whistle work?"

Makayla tells him she thinks it did.

"Any more signs of that mountain lion?" he asks.

The mountain lion.

Makayla had almost forgotten about that.

"Negative on new prints," she answers. "You already know about the carcass from yesterday."

"Stay sharp," Frank says. "And keep in touch."

He doesn't ask what she's doing next, or where she's going. Maybe he doesn't want to know. Maybe he trusts Ranger Devaroix to do the job in the best way she sees fit.

"Over and out," Makayla says.

She looks across the valley, tightens the straps of her pack, and heads out in long, purposeful strides.

[CARTER]

Carter comes to tilted, rocky terrain, with an accumulation of large boulders scattered about the slope, along with low evergreens and dense underbrush.

He keeps looking back, half expecting to see John stalking him. Occasionally, he bends to tie a scrap of red cloth at knee level. He feels the bite of autumn in the air; summer fades fast in the mountains.

A pine cone drops behind him. Startled, Carter spins, sees nothing. It's a claustrophobic feeling he can't shake. Like the clouds sagging down upon his shoulders. The sense he's being followed. There's nothing he can do about it. Just keep moving, hoping that maybe he'll come across a trail, some clue to civilization. He stops, notices scratch marks on the side of a tree. Not made from antlers, the way John had pointed out yesterday. The gouges in this tree were made by claws. Deep grooves run down the bark from the height of shoulder to shins. He imagines his cat at home clawing up the side of the sofa. *A bear*, he figures. He looks around. It's not a safe feeling.

Carter holds the purloined knife in his right hand, squeezes the grip. The wilderness feels immense and inexhaustible. It is relentless. And by now, Carter fully respects its capacity to kill.

He keeps moving.

He desires to get to the spot where he saw that helicopter. An open space. Maybe if he can . . .

A branch snaps.

Carter looks up to see John step out from behind thick brush. He is shirtless, even in this cool air. He's painted two streaks of mud under each eye. The wild man of the mountains. John holds a bow raised to eye level, an arrow pulled all the way back. He is twenty feet away. The expression on his face is stone-cold, lacking all emotion.

Scary John is back.

"John—"

The angular man tilts his head to aim.

Releases his fingers.

[COUGAR]

arter hears but does not see the arrow whiz above his shoulder. He turns at the sound of quaking leaves, a broken branch, then another, and sees the tawny cat fall heavily from tree to ground, John's arrow sticking from its chest.

John swiftly walks past Carter—he's already reloaded—and approaches the fallen cougar, bow drawn. He soon relaxes, lowers the bow, prods the lifeless animal with the toe of his boot. John takes a knee, puts his hand on the animal's side, inclines his head as if in mourning.

Carter watches, stunned.

"Is that a . . . ?"

John turns his head. "Mountain lion, cougar, puma, they're all different names for the same thing. This one's been stalking you for the past ten minutes." John evinces an electric sort of energy, hyped from the kill.

Carter remains speechless, trying to process what's just happened.

"*Puma concolor*, an obligate carnivore," John states, pronouncing the words slowly. "It must eat meat to survive." He rises, studying the animal. "This one killed a fawn yesterday. They are ambush predators, and I'm pretty sure he was getting ready to leap on your back."

"Pretty sure?" Carter echoes.

John pulls on his beard, eyes twinkling. "Did you want me to wait to find out?"

Carter doesn't answer.

John estimates the lion at about seven feet long from nose to tail, 150 pounds.

"Give or take," Carter says.

John nods. "Give or take, yeah. He would have killed you before you ever saw him. The mysterious thing is this: What's it doing here? I'm looking at it, and I still can't believe it."

Carter steps closer. The animal is magnificent. As beautiful as any creature he's ever seen. Small head, rounded ears, white whiskers, slender body, black on the sides of its muzzle and the tip of its surprisingly long tail.

John clamps a strong hand around the back of Carter's neck. "They bite down—right there," he says.

Carter tries to pull away. John grips him for an extra beat, teasingly. He lets go. Grins at the boy. "Mountain lions are out West. There aren't any in the Northeast. Rooted out and wiped out long ago." He bends to lift the big cat's massive front paw. "Guess nobody told this guy."

"You said it was stalking me?" Carter asks.

John nods.

"So you killed it?"

John figures that question doesn't merit a reply.

"You've been following me all this time?" he asks.

John shuts his eyes, exhales out of his mouth. "I was awake when you left."

"You could have stopped me," Carter continues. "Instead, you let me go—and watched over me."

"And I do feel bad about that," John says, indicating the lion. "It was only doing what was natural for it. Just trying to live."

Carter can't help but see the similarities between the man and the lion, both solitary creatures in a hostile world. Rooted out, wiped out. A shame it had to die.

John suddenly lifts his head, turns, square-shouldered, feet wide, and faces an opening in the brush. He grabs Carter by the elbow and pulls him close. The ranger steps forward. They pause in that instant, facing off like two fighters in a steel cage. The ranger is a tall, dark-skinned young woman. She identifies herself in a calm, confident, not unfriendly voice: "I'm Ranger Devaroix. I work for the Department of Environmental Conservation. And I am looking for a boy"—her eyes meet Carter's—"by the name of Carter Taylor."

[INTERVIEW]

I'm Carter," the boy says.

The ranger's eyes flicker from the boy to the man, coldly appraising the dynamic between them. She feels the nervous energy pulsing off the shirtless man, like the vibrations that come from a fishing line when a powerful creature dives to the deep. The bearded man doesn't look directly at her. His eyes dart around, as if searching for a means of escape. He is holding a compound bow in his left hand. It is not loaded. She calculates how long it might take the man to draw back an arrow. There is a dead mountain lion by their feet. Makayla remembers to smile at the boy. Her training calls upon her to defuse the tension. It is also her nature to be calm, direct, friendly. She hopes to strike a delicate balance. Makayla does not want to threaten the wild-eyed man—he appears wired, not quite right, uncomfortable and anxious—yet she must also demonstrate authority and seriousness of purpose.

Being a cop isn't easy.

"Your sister's safe," she tells the boy.

"Grace," he says. As he utters her name, everything about his face and demeanor transforms before the ranger's eyes. Every muscle in his face seems to lift. He stands taller, leans forward. "She's okay?"

"Yes," Makayla says. "She's doing great. We found her last night. She's been air-lifted to safety."

"The helicopter," Carter remembers.

Makayla grins.

The man twitches, gives off an anxious, agitated vibe. He's clearly ill at ease.

Makayla addresses John. Her tone is soft and calm. "I don't know what's going on here, sir. I'm not here to hurt anyone. I just need to put the pieces of the puzzle together."

Carter glances at John. The man's right hand still grips the boy's elbow. The ranger needs to separate them.

"You understand," she says to the man, "I can't talk to you if you are holding that weapon."

John blinks, looks down at the bow in his hand.

"I need for to you put it down and step away," Makayla says. She does not reach for her gun. She purposefully softens every word and gesture. And yet still . . . this is not a request. She means what she says. Everyone knows it.

"It's not loaded," he begins.

"I can see that," Makayla answers. "But we'll all relax if you put it on the ground, sir, please."

John lowers the bow to the ground, and in doing so releases the grip from Carter's arm. He steps to the side.

"Thank you," Makayla says. "I appreciate your trust."

"John saved my life," Carter says. "He found me and—"

Makayla holds up a hand. "I want to hear everybody's side of the story. But first, I need you two to separate." She glances at a tree off to the side, still in her peripheral vision. "Carter, I'd like you to come sit at the base of this tree."

The boy hesitates, then walks to the tree and begins to sit without looking at John.

"On the other side," Makayla says, indicating with her finger. She wants Carter out of the line of fire. She half turns to the boy, not taking her eyes off the man. "You stay right here, Carter, don't move. Wait until I come for you. Right now I'm going to speak privately with this gentleman. Is that all right with you?"

Carter looks up, trusts the ranger, nods. They lock eyes for a moment. Makayla quickly scans his body for signs of bruising, injury, any kind of distress. "Have you been hurt in any way?" she asks.

"No, ma'am," Carter answers.

Makayla steps to the man, inclines her head toward the cougar. "John, is that right?"

He nods, eyes restless.

"I see you did a little hunting today. That's an impressive shot."

They both regard the dead animal.

The man glances warily at the ranger.

"I only care about the boy's safety," Makayla says.

The man stands motionless. He wears no shirt. His body is lean, sinewy, underweight. Tattoos cover both arms and most of his chest. A former soldier, she guesses, after a quick scan of the images. His face appears gaunt, cheeks sunken, making his eyes appear slightly oversize for his skull. His hair is shoulder-length, thinning, with streaks of gray. Even at rest, his body seems coiled. Makayla is careful not to come too close.

"I need you to sit down," she says.

The man wavers, looks to the sky in resignation, closes his eyes, sits.

"Thank you," Makayla says. And, after a pause, "I believe I saw you yesterday."

The man waits. No reaction.

"How long have you been living out here, John?" she asks.

He shrugs.

"I need you to cooperate, sir," Makayla says, her tone sharpening. "That child over there has been missing for six days. This is serious. Do you understand? I need to know exactly how he came to be with you."

John looks up, for the first time meeting her eyes. "I found him collapsed in the bog. I never hurt the boy. I would never do anything like that, ever."

Makayla sees that he is speaking the truth. She points to a tattoo on his right bicep. "Semper fi. You were a marine?"

He gives an involuntary shiver. "Once and forever," he replies.

"Iraq? Afghanistan?" she asks.

He tells her. Slowly, haltingly answers all the ranger's questions.

"Thank you for your sacrifice," she says. "And for what you've done here, for the boy."

He gives no reply.

Makayla says, "You are aware that it's my duty to report this."

"I know."

"You could walk down with us," Makayla offers. "We could sort it out together. Maybe get you some help?"

"That's not agreeable to me," he replies.

It's the answer Makayla anticipated.

"The boy's safety and well-being," she says, pausing until he looks up at her, "is my first priority. I didn't come here looking for you."

The man scratches at the earth with an index finger, listening.

Makayla takes off her hat, runs a hand through her hair. It's decision time. The ranger replaces the hat on her head, pulls the brim low. "Is there anything I can do for you?" she asks.

He looks at the ruined cougar. The magnificent creature the world had conspired against. John tried to imagine its life, the stone-cold miracle of its being here. A mountain lion, here. Those enormous front paws, the blackened coloration around its eyes, the perfect pink triangle of a snout. Her athletic body, so well-proportioned: capable of climbing trees with ease, the ability to pounce forty feet upon a foe. John felt, in comparison, unworthy. And yet he was the vessel of its destruction. He alone had pulled back the bow.

He took the shot that took the life.

John looks back at the ranger.

"What can you do for me?" he repeats, shaking his head. "To be honest? Just leave me be."

It's Makayla's turn to process the request. She takes a card from her wallet. Hands it to him. "That's my number. When you come down from the mountain, John, if there's anything I can do, if you ever need anything at all . . ."

The man holds the card in his hand, flicking it with his thumb.

"The break-ins must stop," the ranger says.

John looks up, a little surprised. He feels a stab of guilt.

"That's not who you want to be in this world," she says. "They will lock you up. Do you understand?"

He signals that he does.

Makayla runs both hands across the back of her neck. The boy is leaning out from behind the tree, watching. "What's your full name?" she asks.

"John," he says. And then as if remembering, recalling a word from long ago, adds, "Riorden."

"Okay, John Riorden," the ranger answers. "Now I'm going to speak with Carter. If he confirms the details of your story, we should be all set. But until that time, I need you to stay seated. You are not free to leave. Is that clear?"

"Yes," he answers.

"Do you trust me, John?" she asks.

A noise comes from his nose. He looks away, shrugs, ducks his head. It's the best he's going to give her.

Of course he doesn't trust her. John doesn't trust anyone.

Makayla goes to the boy.

66

[DARK ANGEL OF THE WOOD]

Before they leave, Carter asks, "Can I say good-bye to him?"

Makayla glances toward the man, still rooted beside the stunted pine. "Sure."

The boy goes to him. "What are you going to do?"

"I'll gather my gear, find a new place," John says.

"You could live with us," Carter says. "Or, like, I don't know, my parents could help you. They have money. And you haven't even met Grace. She's awesome and—"

John rises. He's looking past the boy to the ranger. He wants this to end.

Carter looks at him, bewildered. "I was lost," he says, his voice cracking. "And you found me. You saved me. Twice. Now it's our turn. Let us help you."

John picks up his bow. "You should go."

"But what about you?"

John stiffly puts forth a hand.

Carter takes it. His hand feels small in John's immense, strong grip. They shake once, awkwardly.

John lets go, looks away. "It's the way it is, that's all," he says.

Makayla finally puts a hand on the boy's shoulder, gently pulls him away. "It's time to go home, Carter. You've got family who can't wait to see you."

Carter looks into the bright gray eyes of the ranger. He thinks of Grace, his parents—his dog, Sitka. They turn to walk away. When Carter pauses to look back, John is already gone. Vanished into the forest, a dark angel of the wood.

Was he even real? Carter wonders, not quite believing it could be so.

The boy doesn't talk much on the way down. Makayla doesn't press him, gives him space for his thoughts. He's tired now, feels depleted, as if he could sleep for a hundred days. They stop to sit on a rock ledge. The view is spectacular. Makayla offers him an apple. The juice explodes in his mouth.

She points out a high peak. "That's Blood Mountain. I don't believe you ever got there."

Carter stares at it, repeating the words in silence. *Blood Mountain.* He looks back up in the direction from which they came. John is up there somewhere, padding silently. Good walking leaves no trace.

"Will he be okay?" Carter asks.

Makayla's lips tighten. "I don't know." She pauses, shakes her head.

"He's lost," Carter says.

Makayla nods in agreement.

"Maybe he'll find his way home," Carter offers. But it's more question than comment.

No one pretends to know the answer.

Makayla lifts her head up, breathes in the fresh late-morning air. They say the weather pattern's going to break. The sky already a deep, smooth blue. It's been a long few days. She's tired, too. She brings her arm around the boy's shoulders.

"You ready to go home?" she asks.

"I am," Carter says.

"You want to walk or—?"

"Uber," the boy jokes, face brightening.

Makayla clicks on her radio. Says to Carter, "I may have something even better."

[EPILOGUE]

Grace slides open the glass door to her semirural backyard. Sitka slips through, rarely missing a chance to smell the outdoors. The yard is fenced in all around; she can't go far.

Thwonk.

The dog pads over to Carter, who has set up target practice. His new slingshot arrived today in the mail, along with a box of ammo. Steel balls. Across the yard, he's propped a couple of boards across cinder blocks. Upon them sits various targets: a plastic Clorox container, an array of dented seltzer cans, a number of old action figures looking battered and aggrieved.

Grace moves well now, without pain, though she's still wearing a walking boot. Doesn't need crutches anymore. She had surgery on her ankle a few days after the rescue. Ligament damage. Not the best way to start the school year, though it gives her temporary access to the elevator and an excuse to be late for band, which is all the way on the other side of the building. She still feels a dull ache where two of her ribs were fractured. It's getting better, though.

"Want to try?" Carter offers.

"Sure, I guess," Grace says.

Carter watches her fumble with it for a moment.

"Here, let me show you." Carter places a ball in the center of the leather pouch. He demonstrates as he speaks. "This is a thick band, like the one John uses. For power, you know? You've got to pull it back nice and steady, see? The same way every time. That's the important thing. You have to be consistent with your set up, or else your shot will go all over the place."

"Okay, okay," Grace says impatiently. She doesn't love being schooled by her younger brother. She shoots without any real attention to detail—the ball zips somewhere above the target—she doesn't exactly care where.

Grace hands the slingshot back to her brother. "You're not going to kill anything, are you?" she asks.

"Just Spider-Man," Carter says. He takes a shot, and the ball hits Spidey in the leg, knocking over the action figure.

"I got an email from Makayla," Grace says.

Carter lowers the slingshot. Waits.

"She's so awesome. I want to be her someday," Grace says with a smile.

Carter laughs. "Yeah, she's cool." And after a pause, "Has she heard anything, you know, about John?"

Grace shakes her head.

"Didn't think so," Carter says, and reloads the pouch. "He doesn't want to be found."

"I wish I could have met him," Grace says.

Carter tilts his head. He isn't so sure about that. Releases the shot, misses.

Sitka barks at the glass door. Taps it with the claws of her front paw. Something inside has gotten her attention.

"Dad's home," Grace says, heading toward the door. "You coming in?"

"In a sec," Carter replies.

It's been five weeks since they've come off the mountain. In a way, it's like the whole thing never happened. So easy to slip into a routine of school and sports and phones and gaming. Their father is back to normal, more or less. He's returned to work. Promises to eat better. Takes long walks around the neighborhood with their mom. He even claims he's lost six pounds, like it's some kind of accomplishment. No one believes it. Just Dad being Dad.

Situation normal.

Still, at unexpected times, Carter finds himself thinking of John. The man who saved his life—and terrified him at the same time. *Where is he now?* Carter wonders. *What is he doing?*

Will he ever find peace?

The door slides open a crack, just wide enough for Grace to poke her head through. "Dinner," she says. "Mom made chili."

Carter takes one last shot.

Draws the bow back, lets his hand lightly touch his face.

Tilts his head to aim down the length of his left arm.

Releases his fingers.

Bull's-eye.

ACKNOWLEDGMENTS

I'd like to give special thanks to two members of the New York State Department of Environmental Conservation. The director of the Division of Forest Protection, Eric Lahr, was my first contact when I began delving into this area of research. Not only did Eric take time to patiently answer my many questions about lost hikers and rescue operations, he put me in touch with Ranger Megan McCone, who was generous with her time and enthusiastic, always. Megan and I spoke on the phone, emailed, texted, and sent fat packages back and forth. She was always there for me, going above and beyond anything I could have reasonably asked. Megan's comments and insights helped ground this book in realistic details. Thank you, Ranger McCone. I once was lost, but now I'm found. We still haven't met, but a part of you lives inside this book. I'm so grateful for that.

No book is made without the contributions of countless people. Once again, my editor, Liz Szabla, proved instrumental in her deft touch: when to prompt and shape, when to encourage, when to leave me alone. How does she know? It's a wonder. Liz has a cardsharp's knack for knowing what to hold and what to discard. I came to Liz with a fuzzy idea—but with no map, no compass. Somehow over the course of a long conversation, my vague idea transformed into something substantially different. In other words, Liz showed me True North, set me on the path. Go, write. The wanderings were up to me.

There was a real Sitka, a friend's dog that lived with us for a while in college. But the dog in my mind during the writing of this book was my first, dear Doolin, scooped up from the pound, my loyal companion for many walks through the woods.

Many different books informed and inspired the writing of this one. Four seem especially worthy of acknowledgment: *The Hidden Life of Trees* by Peter Wohlleben, *The Stranger in the Woods* by Michael Finkel, *The Lost Words* by Robert Macfarlane, and *Inside a Dog: What Dogs See, Smell, and Know* by Alexandra Horowitz.

Thanks, lastly, to my family: Lisa, Nick, Gavin, and Maggie. I'd be lost without you.

Thank you for reading this Feiwel & Friends book.
The friends who made **BLOOD MOUNTAIN** possible are:

JEAN FEIWEL
PUBLISHER

LIZ SZABLA
ASSOCIATE PUBLISHER

RICH DEAS
SENIOR CREATIVE DIRECTOR

HOLLY WEST
SENIOR EDITOR

ANNA ROBERTO
SENIOR EDITOR

KAT BRZOZOWSKI
SENIOR EDITOR

VAL OTAROD
ASSOCIATE EDITOR

ALEXEI ESIKOFF
SENIOR MANAGING EDITOR

KIM WAYMER
SENIOR PRODUCTION MANAGER

ANNA POON
ASSISTANT EDITOR

EMILY SETTLE
ASSOCIATE EDITOR

ERIN SIU
EDITORIAL ASSISTANT

KATIE KLIMOWICZ
SENIOR DESIGNER

Follow us on Facebook or visit us online at mackids.com.
Our books are friends for life.